GRIMOLDA GRIZZ
WITCH
EXTRAORDINAIRE

A Witch and Her Cat
Living in Today's World

By
Avril Gilmore Blamire

ISBN-13: 978-1519550996
ISBN-10: 1519550995

CONTENTS

for absi
with love
and
best wishes
from
avril

ACKNOWLEDGMENTS

My heartfelt thanks to Antonia Bunch for her encouragement, support and enthusiasm, not least being her concern for Grimpuss's welfare!

To David Walls for his encouragement, enthusiasm and I.T. know-how which sent me in the right direction.

Chapter One

Grimolda Grizz had a problem – how to adjust to the modern world. She had experienced centuries of enjoyable living. She had been free to do what she liked, where she liked, when she liked. And she had had power, power over hordes of simple souls who went in awe of her. A cushy life it had been – interesting and invigorating. Until the 21th century came along, and things had gone from bad to worse.

Where before she had lived in seclusion in a vast gloomy wood in the middle of nowhere, now her wood was surrounded by houses and people. Suburbia they called it! What had once been a small village some distance away, and had stayed small for centuries as no-one wanted to live near a witch, had in less fearful times grown and grown and nibbled away at the dark edges of her wood, and no-one knew now that she was a witch, just thought she was a cranky old recluse... which suited Grimolda fine.

Certainly it could encroach no farther as it had

now reached her last defence – the high, creeper-choked wall that surrounded what had once been her innermost sanctuary. And no-one had tried to question her ownership of that murky area.

She was now harassed, however, with letters of complaint, and petitions from the suburbanites of Newtown, asking her to chop down her trees, or at least remove the ones that overshadowed their little gardens, which were always sunk in gloom, no matter what part of the sky the sun happened to favour.

And she had another problem – trespassers. Children, who loved to climb her twisted trees and explore the darkest corners of her wood. But she had been able to deal with them so far. A bat or two sent out to flap at them or a few attacks by Grimpuss, her cat, soon sent them packing with delicious shivers of fear running up and down their spines and screams of excited terror trailing in their wake. But it didn't prevent them coming back for more, so they were an awful nuisance.

Not only was there this intrusion of her privacy, but she was no longer able to travel freely abroad. She had been in the habit of flying off on her broomstick to visit her cousins – Grimalice in Greenland, Grimaggie, and Grimethel who lived at the North Pole, or Grimolive who, at 100 miles away, was nearest. Now she frequently got blown off course by jumbo jets, if not actually chased by them for miles. If, on the other hand, she got into their air stream, she could put her feet up and go into automatic pilot, and have a nap, so it wasn't all bad.

And sometimes she found herself near an airport and hitched a lift on the wing of one going in the right direction, but that was pretty draughty and uncomfortable, and if she wasn't careful she was liable to be blown off!

Worst of all, really, was the boredom, the inactivity, the feeling that she was prisoner in her own world. In fact, it wasn't *her* world any more.

Nobody wanted spells anymore. Nobody wanted their friends turned into frogs for a laugh, or their enemies burned to a frazzle. Nobody wanted potions to make some people ugly or others beautiful. There seemed to be no demand for handsome princes or pretty princesses. Her kind of magic was old-fashioned, out of date. People had their own magic these days – radios, television, rockets and spaceships, and they seemed to be too independent to want potions and spells. Bumping people off was now a do-it-yourself matter.

In the end she went into the town and bought a television. It wasn't quite 'if you can't beat 'em, join 'em', more an attempt to at least alleviate the boredom that had set in as a result of all this enforced inactivity.

But, a week later, as she sat in front of the set, drumming her fingers on the chair arm, she was very disgruntled. The television screen offered nothing of interest and she was even more bored. How could she have possibly imagined that this silly little box would solve everything?

Her mind wandered back to the main problem. What was she to do? She no longer had any drive or ambition. She was just wasting away, not a pretty sight. Should she put some ads in the paper? 'Grimolda Grizz, witch. Spells, potions, conversions. Effective and quick service.'

Fat lot of use that would be. People would just laugh and say she was an old crank and off her trolley. No-one anymore believed she really was a witch. Besides, it was demeaning and demoralising to advertise herself as a servant to the public, she who had been held in awe in the past, who had been used to being begged for help, not called out casually like an electrician or a plumber. No, that would be unbearable.

She could still make potions for her own benefit, and cast the odd spell on neighbours who had become too nosey for their own good, but there was no work satisfaction in that, and it took up hardly any time at all.

So here she was sulking and grimbling and grumbling in front of this silly little box which seemed to be adding to her boredom instead of alleviating it, when some bright colours jumping about on the screen caught her eye. Not another snooker championship! But despite herself her eyes darted all over the screen in pursuit of the brightly coloured balls. What a lot of idiots these human beings were, inventing all sorts of ways to knock silly little balls about. It was like a child with a rattle. They had to have something to play with.

The clumsy clot at the end of the cue at that moment seemed to be getting nowhere fast – he'd just potted the white! And he looked sick, if that's possible of a snooker player, who's usually bred suave, cool and unruffled.

When his turn came round again, almost without thinking Grimolda narrowed her eyes in concentration then blinked hard, and lo and behold, the right ball dropped into the right pocket and the poor chap smiled weakly in relief and played on. The witch wasn't quite sure whether this really had anything to do with her, so she blinked a few more times and it certainly seemed to work. She tried a few bloomers just to put the lid on it, and chortled with glee as the balls trundled neatly wherever she directed. She was beginning to enjoy herself. She had found a new outlet for her talents. Not once had she imagined that she might have any control over what went on in other parts of the world, just because she could see it happening on a television screen (her crystal ball which had been quite useful in the past had got broken by Grimpuss when in a playful mood, and nobody seemed to make them any more).

An expression which was quite unseemly for a witch flitted momentarily across her face, and she leaned over and touched the set. Why, she'd actually become quite fond of it all of a sudden!

Her new protégé's face appeared in close-up as the camera zoomed in on his now exultant mood. Something about him appealed to her. He had a weaselly look which made him rather attractive and, as his name came up – Ratty – she could see she'd made a good choice. A good, reliable name, worthy to stand with the Blackadders, Snakeleys, Frogginses, Beetles, and Moles of this world.

The match continued. After a bit she began to blink for the other fellow, just to give the weaselly one a qualm or two – being a typical witch, she was partial to these nasty turns of mind – and indulged in a snigger or two, as his newfound composure started to crumble, but she didn't let him slide back too far. After all, she *was* rooting for him. She kept pulling him back in the nick of time, and finally let him win with a flourish amid cheers from the audience. He and his opponent were in a state of collapse, and as the cameras took in the scene, the entire company looked wrung out like wet rags. What a lovely sight!

Grimolda patted the set as she switched it off, and went to make herself a good strong brew of mulled snake venom, with a leer on her face that almost split it in two. In passing she bent to stroke Grimpuss, who leapt away in horror at this infringement of witchly behaviour.

As she sat in her kitchen, holding the steaming mug in her horny hands, and breathing in the obnoxious fumes, it suddenly hit her that she was no longer bored. Life had got going again for her and the little black box had brought into it another dimension altogether.

After that, Grimolda took to playing havoc with all sorts of games and sports that were presented live on television. She found she had the knack of getting the hang of a game within seconds of watching it, even if she'd never come across it before. And it was very good practice for her powers of observation and concentration, which hadn't been brilliant at the start but were now nothing short of perfection.

She rattled through the darts matches – a welcome change from the never-ending ball games – and the tennis, golf, football, and rugby. The last three weren't so successful. There was a fly in the ointment! If she couldn't see the whole pitch or course, she really had no idea where she was directing the ball and she soon found that guessing had disastrous results, so she had to be contented with playing only when she got the whole scene in perspective. But when she did, did she score some beauties!! At one point she got so carried away that she began to wonder if she could become the first ALL ROUND WORLD CHAMPION OF ALL EXISTING SPORTS, if she actually went and took part in them. But that was short lived – she had no desire for publicity. She much preferred this very private way of turning the world upside down.

Another factor in this new situation was an unfortunate one – perhaps not for her, but certainly for the rest of the world! She was not at all consistent. She would get fed up with one programme halfway through and switch over to another to see what she could do with it. With the result that the participants never knew whether they were, as they'd thought, going through a good patch or a bad patch, and their backers were equally bamboozled.

It came to a climax one day when, while watching Wimbledon, her attention wandered, caught by the antics of Grimpuss as he played with the pet tarantula. When she turned again to the screen she found she'd sent the ball in quite the wrong direction so with a quick blink she altered its flight. As the crowd gasped, the ball seemed to hover in mid air and then go off at a tangent in the opposite direction to land inside the line and win the match. "A freak twist of wind," said the commentator, but Grimolda realised that she was beginning to carry it too far. To play the game within the laws of possibility was fine, but this was a bit much, for these humans' sensibilities anyway. Strangely Grimolda had a teeny weeny bit of fair play in her makeup. Enough was enough. Perhaps she was letting this gadget take over, instead of just contribute to her lifestyle. She had a lot to thank it for but there was no need to wallow in it. Perhaps she should give it a rest for a while. Even the newspapers' fortune tellers had been writing how the 'stars' were affecting the stars!

Chapter Two

'The Nettles', Spookey Heath, was not everybody's idea of an attractive address, thought the postman as he walked up the long dark drive. In fact it couldn't possibly be *anybody's* idea of an attractive address. Why the old lady had kept the name when she bought the place he would never know, unless she had given it that name herself. Come to think of it, from what he had seen of the old lady, it wouldn't surprise him. He pushed a low-hanging branch out of his way. It was more of an obstacle course than a walk. Potholes and boulders forced a hop skip and jump gait on anyone rash enough to venture in there, the hop skip and jump being interspersed with swear words as it was also so dark that the potholes often looked like boulders and the boulders like potholes. The trees reached across above him and tangled themselves up in each other, so that hardly a chink of daylight got through. The whole place was steeped in gloom.

But Pete the postman was used to it, so he didn't

bat an eyelid when dark shapes flapped about in the shadows among the trees, or squeaks and rattles were heard in the undergrowth. He was more concerned with getting to his destination without the added disadvantage of a sprained ankle.

He studied the parcel curiously as he lifted the heavy iron door knocker. He always had to knock on the door even if he only had letters or circulars to deliver, as the old lady didn't have a letter box. That was another daft thing. It would save her all that trailing back and forward if she had one put in. Some people were so stuck in the past they made life more difficult for themselves.

"Time you got that path seen to, or the trees cut back – one or t'other, Miss Grizz, or I'll need danger money to come here," remarked Pete cheerily as the door creaked open a few inches and he got a glimpse of the old lady in the shadows.

"Hmph," was the brief reply, as she reached out and snatched the parcel from his outstretched hand, retreated, and slammed the door in his face.

"Moody old bag," muttered Pete, and he set off back down the drive. "Still, what can you expect? Living like that, stuck away all by herself. And maybe she hasn't any money to improve the place, in which case no wonder she snapped my nose off." He stuck his hands in his pockets and absent-mindedly started whistling as he battled along. Suddenly there was a wild screech high above him. He stopped and screwed up his eyes in an effort to distinguish one thing from another in the gloom. Two green eyes glared back at him. It was a huge black cat.

"Hi puss. Puss, puss, puss," called Pete, who was fond of cats, but the cat didn't seem impressed; it started spitting at him, and showed a vicious-looking tongue which also looked green. *Must be the light*, thought Pete, or had it eaten something that hadn't agreed with it? The next minute he nearly lost his balance as a black body landed on his shoulder with incredible weight and at the same instant gave him a biff on the side of his head that sent his cap spinning. And then it was gone, so fast that he didn't see where. It seemed to just fly away and all he could hear was a distant screech that sounded more human than cat, and a lot of rustling and rattling in the depths of the wood. He picked his cap up, brushed it off, put it on, and continued on his way. By the time he reached his van, on the main road, he had forgotten the incident. He was unaware of the glinting green eyes that had followed him all the way, as Grimpuss flew from tree to tree in pursuit. As Pete drove away, the cat sat on a high branch with a leer on its face and its green tongue flashed greedily round its lips in imagination of what it might have done and anticipation of what it could still do next time.

Meanwhile 'Miss' Grizz was standing at her kitchen table looking at the contents of the parcel with an expression of extreme distaste on her face. It was a mail order catalogue, full of glossy pictures of the most hideous clothes she'd ever seen, all in horrible light, bright colours, and being modelled by a variety of people she found quite repulsive to look at. She turned to the accompanying letter in curiosity, to find that it was from her cousin Grimolive.

"Dear Grimolda," she read. "Haven't heard from

you for a while, so I thought I would get in touch, and at the same time take the opportunity to send you one of my catalogues. I'm afraid I've hit on hard times somewhat, so I'm hoping you will help me out by ordering some things. The commission I get helps to almost make ends meet and it keeps me occupied too – gives me something to do. I really was feeling pretty redundant before. Hope you're faring better. Looking forward to hearing from you, Grimolive."

Grimolda tutted away under her breath as she flicked through the pages of the catalogue. Her cousin must really be in a bad way to have been reduced to this, and at that instant she made up her mind to go and see Grimolive. There was no way she could bring herself to order any of these revolting things. The only way she might be able to help would be to go and talk her out of this, and perhaps suggest an alternative course. "Like the blind leading the blind," she grumbled to herself, but still there might be a chance.

She told Grimpuss, who was quite pleased to have something different to do, and went over to collect her broomstick which stood in the corner behind the back door, but when she opened the door she stopped short. She had been so eager to get away she'd forgotten it was broad daylight, and a witch just couldn't flit about during the day. She would have to wait until night time, so she sat back down, and while she sat she tried to think of what poor Grimolive could possibly do, but by the time dusk approached she had only got herself into a fidgety state, while Grimpuss sat and watched her and bit his nails, a habit he had got into of late, being very sensitive to his mistress's moods.

At least it now seemed dark enough to go, and with a sigh of relief the witch gathered together herself, her cat, and her broomstick, and set off.

As Grimolda soared above the trees and away from Spookey Heath her mood changed. The chilly air and the harsh blackness of the night began to have a revitalising effect. The moon appeared from behind the clouds and, out of the darkness below, rivers glimmered and glowed. Thin wisps of smoke hung in the air above slated roofs, and lights sparkled from windows and street lamps. Occasionally a car travelled along a road, looking like a glow worm from Grimolda's lofty viewpoint.

It was quite some time since Grimolda had sallied forth among the world, and she was enjoying it. Her broomstick had been gathering dust for far too long.

She flew nonchalantly over miles and miles of countryside, some just as she had remembered it, and some so changed that she thought she had gone off course, until another patch of familiarity appeared below to reassure her. Towns spilled untidily all over the place; villages that had once been self-contained tagged onto each other in a haphazard fashion. But the countryside itself was much the same as before – farmland, woodland, hills and dales – they would never change?

Grimolda was waxing philosophical – she didn't relish over-civilisation.

When she arrived at Grimolive's part of the world she had not only enjoyed her journey but she was also keyed up with excitement at the thought of seeing her cousin again. *And how pleased she'll be to see me too, the poor soul,* thought Grimolda, as she alighted on the ground and, giving her broomstick and Grimpuss, who had fallen asleep, a brisk shakedown, she approached Grimolive's hut. Grimolive had never been one for luxury and the mingy, dingy little hut looked worse than it had ever done. There was a hole in the roof and the door appeared to be half off its hinges. *She's in an even worse state than she's let on,* thought Grimolda as she banged on the door. No answer. The witch pushed at the door and it opened, creaking. *Not even bothered any more about security. Hmphh!*

Grimolda went in. The interior of the hut was worse than the exterior. It was dreadful, even to a witch's sensibilities. Everything was so thick with dust, she could hardly make out what it was that was actually under the dust.

It came to her at last that the place had not been visited, never mind lived in, for a very long time. But where was Grimolive?

Grimolda stepped back outside and looked around. The wood was tight packed around her and now she could see that there was no longer a path leading through it to the hut. Grimolive was obviously nowhere near.

With absolutely no idea how she was going to find her now, the witch took off once more. She didn't even know if Grimolive had put her new address on her letter; she hadn't bothered to look. More fool she!

She started flying around the wood in ever widening circles, hoping to get a clue, and getting more grumpy and mumpy by the minute. The wood just kept on sitting there like a big black beast, giving nothing away. But as her circles widened it began to thin out and become dotted with houses, and in no time she was flying over a town. It looked for all the world like Newtown – suburbia all over again. *It's happening everywhere,* thought Grimolda, and she was about to give up and go home when she became aware of a dense cloud of green smoke coming in short, sharp blasts from one of the chimneys beneath.

Funny, thought Grimolda, *that's just like a signal.* She swooped lower, and the green smoke kept belching out, gradually engulfing the whole area.

As she descended through the green blanket towards the house it was coming from, the door opened and a blonde woman in a bright pink dressing gown appeared on the step. Grimolda was about to fly away when a familiar voice yelled, "Mouldy, Mouldy, it's me, it's me!" And it was! It was Grimolive.

Chapter Three

Grimolda hovered, struck dumb by the vision beneath her. She stared with blatant disbelief – it was her cousin's face all right, but the rest of her was something else! A brightly yellow, blonde, permed frizz of hair bobbed above the grinning features, and beneath them the revolting pink dressing gown was brighter than ever in close-up. Billowing out from under it were the skirts of a frilly nightie and, below that, pink fluffy slippers. And as her cousin held out her hands – pink nail varnish!

"Come in, come in!" cried Grimolive's voice. "I saw you a minute or two ago as I was putting the cat out, and I was so afraid I wouldn't catch you, but I remembered the old frog slime smoke signal powder and threw some on the fire right away, and thank goodness – it worked!"

Goodness, goodness, thank goodness? What sickly sweetness. This was becoming more of a nightmare every second. She weakly followed her cousin into the house. It was revolting! Anything that wasn't pink was shining white, or cream, or pale blue.

"Sit down, sit down," cackled Grimolive happily, obviously oblivious to her cousin's state of shock. "I'll make you a nice cup of coffee – won't be a min."

Grimolda collapsed into a big soft couch, and looked around for Grimpuss for support, but the cat was nowhere to be seen. *No wonder*, thought Grimolda, *he's got more sense*. She wished she could just head for home, but she had to find out what dreadful calamity had befallen her cousin, no matter how horrified and nauseated she felt. And perhaps she could still help to extricate Grimolive from this terrible mess. She could hear her cousin singing – *singing* – brightly and tunefully in the kitchen, and in a minute she was back with a tray neatly set out with mugs of steaming coffee, milk jug, sugar bowl and biscuit box – all bright pink.

"This *is* a surprise," she gabbled. "It's great to see you but what brought you here? I expected to get a letter in answer to mine, not to actually see you. Don't get me wrong, it's great to see you. I'm delighted. It's been so long."

"Well yes," said Grimolda, wondering how to word her reply. "I've not been away from home much for a while and I just took a notion to come and see how you're getting on."

"Well anyway, it's lovely to see you," gushed Grimolive, smiling at her cousin in such a sweet and sickly way that it was all that Grimolda could do to stay in her seat. The coffee tasted revolting, the place was revolting, her cousin was getting more revolting by the minute.

"You must stay for a day or two." Grimolive's sweet voice broke into her thoughts.

"Oh no! No, thanks very much all the same. It... it... really it was all on the spur of the moment, and I'll have to go back... Too much to do at home," babbled Grimolda in a state of panic.

"Oh that's too bad. Still, you must come back soon. Promise?"

"Oh yes, very soon," said Grimolda, lying in her teeth. Then, taking the bull by the horns, she said, "Actually, I really came to see if I could help you get out of this mess."

"Mess, what mess?" said Grimolive with big round eyes.

"Well this..." Words failed her and trailed away into silence. She made another brave attempt. "You said you had come on bad times."

"Oh that. Oh yes," said Grimolive quite cheerfully. "Oh it's working out fine now. I was a bit down when I wrote to you, certainly, but everything's all right now. I got this nice little council house, you see, and the neighbours have been so kind and helpful. I know it was strange at first but now I've almost forgotten my old life. This is so much more cosy and comfortable and it's lovely having friends all around me – you don't know what you're missing... What's the matter?"

Grimolda in one bound had reached the door and was struggling frantically with the door knob. "I must go," she blabbered, "I really must – I've stayed too long already!"

And she wrenched open the door and fled, ignoring her cousin's cries of "Come back!" and, "What about my order book? Don't you want any nice clothes or anything?" and then, when she found she was talking to herself! "What on earth can have upset her so badly? It must have been seeing me so happy here in my nice little house. What a shame. I didn't mean to make her jealous. Oh poor Grimolda!" And she turned back to her nice little house with a sad shake of her head, and locked up for the night.

Grimolda was in a terrible state of shock. She had no idea how she had managed to find her way home. She had absolutely no recollection of the journey and it was only now that she was becoming aware of her surroundings that she realised she was actually home. How long she had been sitting in her chair in the kitchen she couldn't tell. On the table at her side stood an empty bottle of deadly nightshade wine and an empty glass. The clock on the mantelpiece had stopped, but then it was never the right time anyway as she only wound it up to hear its rickety ticking and never bothered to alter the hands. She didn't normally need to know the time...

It was pitch black outside, so it was night time, but she knew in her bones it wasn't the same night; she was stiff with cold and with being in the same position for a very long time. She sighed and, getting up from her chair, moved slowly over to the fire, struck a match, and got it going. She sank back onto her knees in front of the sparky glow and absent-mindedly rubbed her hands and gazed into the black depths. It was as if she'd awakened from a nightmare. Had it really been real – that dreadful experience? Had her cousin gone completely off her rocker? What a terrible way to go!

The silence behind her began to sink into her senses. There was something else wrong with it apart from the clock's lack of tick. She was quite alone in the room. Where was Grimpuss? Come to think of it, the last time she had seen her cat, he was sitting in front of her on the broomstick, as she had come down to land at Grimolive's. In a sudden panic she leapt to the door and yanked it open, yelling, "Grimp, Grimp!" at the top of her voice. There was an answering cacophony of sound as mice squeaked, bats flapped, and various others of her livestock responded in one way or another – but no Grimpuss.

She had left him behind! She started cursing him for not seeing in time that she had been going to leave, and for not being ready to go with her, but it was only out of frustration, for she knew that at the rate at which she had fled from Grimolive's there was no way he could have been ready unless he had been sitting right on the broomstick!

She knew Grimpuss could take care of himself anywhere, she wasn't worried on that score. But she would have to go back for him. He was too far away to come home on his own. She couldn't see him going anywhere near her cousin for help – he hadn't even stood that sight as long as she had. She just couldn't leave him for long in such a hostile place, so, reluctant as she was, she got out her broomstick and set off again. This time she didn't notice the landscape beneath her or anything much other than the landmarks that were to get her to Grimolive's. Truth to tell, there wasn't a lot to see, as this time there was no moon and it took her all her time to pick out the familiar landmarks. Twice she found she was off course and had to retrace her flight.

At last the lights of the nasty little town appeared, twinkling on the horizon and, as she drew nearer, her heart sank to her boots and her hands started shaking. To go through that experience again so soon was almost too much for her. But she made a tremendous effort and carried on and soon she was directly above her cousin's house. She had been hoping that she would immediately see Grimpuss sitting on the roof waiting for her, in which case they could have got away with hardly a scar. But there was no sign of the cat and as she looked around her everything was becoming more clearly visible. Dawn was breaking, and with a sinking heart she realised she would have to spend a whole day with Grimolive. She let out a screech of terror at the thought. No, she would never set foot in that horrid place as long as she lived. She would have to find shelter for the day and come back at night.

She set off again and started exploring the immediate neighbourhood, and after a minute or two she saw a large wooden hut with a black tarred roof, standing on a piece of waste ground. It seemed quite deserted, so she floated down to the back of it where there was a scruffy little patch of trees, and landing, she made her way stealthily towards the hut. After peering in all the windows she was quite satisfied that it really was empty. She had to break a window at the back to get in, and she sank gratefully onto a wooden chair in what appeared to be a cupboard full of chairs, and promptly fell fast asleep, weak with exhaustion.

She slept and slept and slept and slept. At one point she half surfaced, aware that she was hungry and thirsty but, unable to summon up enough energy to actually wake and go looking for food, she sank back into a heavy stupor.

Out of this she finally wakened with a start. To be more accurate she jumped out of her skin. A sound, the like of which she had never heard before, had started on the other side of the door.

Chapter Four

Terrified, she crouched behind the pile of chairs with her hands over her ears. The sound went on and on, varying only in intensity and pitch. Sometimes it was an ear-splitting scream, sometimes a hoarse roar. What sort of frightening beast this was she just could not imagine; it was obviously in a towering rage, as underneath the roar came a steady thumping, as if it was pawing the ground with great hard hooves.

Normally Grimolda was unaffected by animals of any kind, being used to a variety of nasty beasts, but this was strange and powerful and totally unnerving. After a while she began to stop shaking. The noise hadn't altered. It did stop for a minute but then it started again. It had come no nearer, but neither had it retreated. She couldn't just stay there forever. She would have to do something. After all she could escape through the broken window behind her. But there might be more of these monsters outside at this very minute, lying in wait silently. She couldn't see a thing, it was pitch black, so yet again she must have slept through the whole day.

In the end curiosity got the better of her. At least she would like to know what was terrifying her so. She crept over to the door and looked through the keyhole. To her amazement all she could see was half a dozen youths in the middle of the room jumping up and down banging things and surrounded by a lot of black boxes. And then it came to her that she had heard something similar before on her TV set, and the people had called it a 'group'. But this was so loud and reverberating so much it was almost lifting the roof off. And it was so close it was trying to blast her ears off. And it was so awful that it was making her feel sick.

Some of the stuff they called music on the telly she enjoyed, especially the kind produced by the people they called punks. They appealed to her a lot – in fact she had often wondered if they had a bit of witch blood in them, they bore such a strong resemblance to her kind and on the whole she liked the sounds they produced. But this, this was something else! She had calmed down now that she knew she had nothing to fear, but she had to get away, as her ears were ringing, her head was aching and she was feeling more nauseated by the minute. She climbed out through the window, and made her way to where she had left her broomstick propped against a tree. It wasn't there! She dashed from tree to tree but it just wasn't there.

A noise in the distance attracted her attention and as she turned towards it a light flared up at the other end of the waste ground and started moving wildly around. She wasn't in much doubt as to what was causing it and her fears were confirmed as she crept from tree to tree towards it. Three lads were dancing around shouting a sort of war cry and passing from one to another – her broomstick, which had now turned into a flaming torch. She sank to the ground at the foot of a tree and sagged against it.

She was stranded! What on earth was she to do? How on earth was she going to get home? The seconds seemed to freeze as she sat hugging her knees and rocking backward and forward in a state of misery. Eventually she got wearily to her feet, realising that there was no alternative but to go and seek out Grimolive, and ask her help.

As she walked along the pavements under the lamplight, people approaching either looked at her askance and steered clear of her, or crossed the road before she reached them. She didn't even have her hat on, which normally had an unnerving effect on people; she had left it at home in her hurry to get away. But she was used to being avoided and on she strode, her long black cloak almost trailing on the ground and her long grey hair flapping round her shoulders.

Her good sense of direction got her to Grimolive's fairly quickly, and she hammered on the door. Sounds of music from inside faded and a light came on in the hall. The door opened and there stood Grimolive, this time in a shocking pink dress which exposed her bony knees, high-heeled white shoes, and a bright pink ribbon in her frizzy golden hair.

"Mouldy!" she exclaimed with obvious delight.

"Oh I am so glad to see you, dear. I was so worried when you dashed off so sudden like. Do come in," and she caught hold of Grimolda's hands and pulled her into the house. A cloying sickly sweet perfume hung in the air around her.

Grimolda nearly ran away again. It was only her total dependence on her cousin's assistance that got her into the house. She let herself be led into the sitting room, only to come abruptly to a standstill as a figure rose from the settee.

"Oh Arthur," babbled Grimolive gaily, "this is my cousin Grimolda. Remember I told you she called in in passing the other day. I didn't expect to see her again for ages. Isn't it lovely that she's come back!" She turned to Grimolda. "Mouldy dear, this is Arthur, a friend who lives down the road. We met at the local social." She turned back to him. "We've always called Grimolda Mouldy," she giggled.

Arthur stepped forward and shook Grimolda's hand heartily, his smile becoming slightly fixed as he peered into her face through the thick lenses of his spectacles.

"Happy to meet you, I'm sure," he mumbled, and sat down again rather hastily.

"Do sit down dear, I'll go and put the kettle on," and Grimolive bustled through to the kitchen.

"Do you live near here?" enquired Arthur politely after a short silence.

"About a hundred miles away," said Grimolda.

"What a long journey you've had then," said Arthur. "Have you come by car or train? We certainly didn't hear you coming up the road."

"Well I..."

"She hasn't got a car," Grimolive's voice interrupted hastily from the kitchen. "I guess she must have come by bus as usual, did you, Mouldy?" Now her cousin's face appeared in the doorway nodding at her emphatically.

"Oh... oh... yes, yes, of course," stammered Grimolda, taking the hint.

"Olive always says she's too nervous to ever drive a car," said Arthur, smiling at Grimolive. "Does it run in the family perhaps?"

"Yes," said Grimolda, and retreated still farther into the chair she had perched on, wishing that the nightmare that now enveloped her would speed up a bit so that she could get to the end of it.

Grimolive came cheerily back into the room with a laden tray, and proceeded to dish out coffee and cream cakes. Before Grimolda could protest she had ladled two spoonsful of sugar into the cup before she handed it over. Grimolda forced down the sugary coffee and the sugary cakes, feeling more miserable by the minute, as her cousin put the record player on again and chatted away brightly to Arthur, who had become quite subdued. *I didn't realise he was so shy with strangers,* Grimolive thought, *but that's really quite a nice quality!*

At long last the coffee was finished and Arthur rose to leave.

"Glad to have met you, er... er... Mouldy," he said as he shook hands and thought, *What an appropriate name*. There was a distinct aura of mould about Mouldy at close quarters.

Grimolive waved a cheerful goodbye and turned back into the house. "He's lovely, isn't he?" she babbled enthusiastically. "I'm so glad I met him. And he seems to like me too. I've been *so* lucky since I came here." She looked pityingly at her less fortunate cousin, and then, with a flash of inspiration, "Why don't you come and live with me here, Mouldy? We could have a lovely time together. And it would be so much nicer for you than that dreary house of yours."

Mouldy shuddered at the thought. "No, no," she protested, "I'm perfectly all right where I am."

Now at last her cousin became curious. "And tell me, what has brought you back so soon?"

"I left Grimpuss behind. I don't know why," mumbled Mouldy, "but somehow he wasn't around when I left and I was home before I realised he wasn't there."

"Oh poor Grimpuss," exclaimed Grimolive, "and I had no idea. I haven't seen him at all, and I don't think Grimy's seen him either, have you?" and she turned to her cat, who was sitting on top of the loudspeaker up on the wall. He shook his head and sneered. He was not overfond of Grimpuss and couldn't have cared less what happened to him.

"And – and – there's another problem," said Grimolda, taking the plunge. "I've lost my broomstick as well."

And the whole story spilled out.

"But Mouldy, what on earth were you doing in the

hut in the first place?"

"Well um... I felt awfully tired, and... er... had got a bit lost and... er... thought I would stop for a rest," lied Grimolda frantically. She couldn't really tell Grimolive that she found her cousin's new image and way of life totally repulsive, and had been running away.

"Oh you poor dear," said Grimolive sympathetically, thinking, *Not only is her memory going, she's getting senile. Maybe it's just as well she doesn't want to join me here.*

"Well, never mind, I've still got my old broomstick out in the tool shed," she said comfortingly. "You can have it and keep it. I'm sure I won't ever need it again. Arthur doesn't know, but I'm going to take driving lessons and surprise him. And of course, you must stay the night, dear."

Grimolda's heart sank once more to her boots, but what could she do?

"I'll go and get the broomstick and give it a dust for you, and we can shout for Grimpuss at the same time."

But there was no reply to their calls and no sign of the cat anywhere.

Grimolive went into the shed and Grimolda sank onto a garden seat. Next minute there was a muffled exclamation and Grimolive appeared at the door looking puzzled. "It's gone!" she exclaimed. "But I don't understand. It's been there ever since I arrived here."

Grimolda dashed in and rummaged about, but sure enough there was no broomstick. Now she *would* have to stay, and another thought struck her. *For how long?!*

As they were walking back to the house, Grimolive prattling happily and Mouldy sunk in gloom, there was suddenly a whirring sound from above, and as they looked up, a dark shape flew over the roof top and came down to land in front of them. Mouldy couldn't believe her eyes. It was Grimpuss. And Grimolive couldn't believe *her* eyes. It was *her* broomstick that Grimpuss was sitting on.

Grimpuss was in a towering rage and it was a while before they could get him to use language that they could understand. It turned out that when he found that he'd been abandoned he hadn't known what to do. He didn't want to see either Grimolive or Grimy, and as he didn't mince his words in explanation, tears of hurt appeared in Grimolive's eyes – so he had retired to the shed to think about what to do, and there in front of him was a broomstick, so with a miaow of relief he grabbed it and set off home.

Unfortunately his sense of direction in the air was not as good as on the ground and he had paid no attention to the route they had taken coming, so it had taken him a day and a night to get home, and when he finally arrived, tired and disgruntled, there was no mistress to welcome him, just cooling ashes in the grate. And so he'd come back, not knowing what could have happened to Grimolda or where she could have gone, and getting almost as lost on the return journey. He had been travelling non-stop for 44 hours and he was a very bad-tempered cat.

Grimolive was in tears because of what he'd said about her and her cat. Grimolda was so relieved at having her cat back *and* transport home, that she could have hugged and kissed even Arthur if he'd been there! At the same time her pent-up feelings made her want to blurt out what *she* felt about Grimolive and her new lifestyle, but she knew she couldn't. After all, it was Grimolive's broomstick.

So she attempted to soothe and appease her cousin, and gave Grimpuss a row which made him sulk for days, and took off straightaway for home in exultant mood. Once she was out of earshot she couldn't stop cackling and screeching with laughter and joy, while Grimpuss sat behind her in a black silence.

Back in her house Grimolive poured herself a neat whisky and sank thankfully into a chair, finally very relieved that her cousin had gone.

"She still hasn't bought any of my nice clothes either," she complained. But she knew she would make no more attempts to make her cousin a customer, or try to persuade her to come and live with her. And she and Grimy sat and gazed into the firelight, thanking their stars that they had had a *very* lucky escape.

Chapter Five

Grimolda straightened her back painfully and looked at her handiwork. She'd let her vegetable garden go to rack and ruin recently and it had taken her ages to rid quite a small area of the flowers which had been trying to take over from her weeds and vegetables. However, things were now beginning to look a bit better and a day or two more would get it all sorted out, and broomstick shape! The sour potatoes hadn't come to any harm, but the creeping cucumber and the spotted cabbage were looking decidedly weak and woebegone.

Her main problem these days was not actually getting them to grow better but knowing what to do with them once they had grown! She had a shed full of them at the moment – racks of green turnips, boxes of squashy purple tomatoes, all separately wrapped in cobwebs to keep them from going too rotten, trays of furry fungus laid out to dry, and bunches of green garlic hanging from hooks in the ceiling. As she put away her tools for the day, she stood at the door and looked at it all. She would never get through that lot on her own in a month of Moondays. But what was she to do? She had no friends to give it to, but she didn't want to waste all this good food.

And then it came to her. That morning a letter had arrived – more a circular really – from the 'newly formed Residents' Association'. It had started off by mentioning that people were invited to make available for general use, on loan of course, whatever tools, machines or implements they possessed that other people might not have. For example a rotivator, a grass roller, a telescopic ladder, etc. And a list would be circulated, of the names and telephone numbers of the willing lenders; a copy of this would be posted up in the Post Office. It went on to say that the Residents' Association would like to raise funds in order to have a Kitty ("Kitty?!") which could be used to finance parties, concerts, or general social functions. The first function they intended putting on was a barbecue in Farmer Brown's field on Bonfire Night.

Donations of food, drink or money would mean that all the entrance money collected would be pure profit and would go into the Kitty. A letter was enclosed from the organiser of the proposed barbecue. By this time Grimolda had decided that the Kitty in these humans' terms couldn't be a cat. People *were* peculiar! They probably meant piggy bank, but again why they had "piggy banks" was also very obscure, as neither cats nor pigs were normally receptacles for money. Once or twice she had heard the phrase 'pigs will fly' used. Sometimes she thought people were really quite brainless. She might be able to make a pig fly, but she doubted if they could!!

Now she had a brainwave. She would donate some of her store to the barbecue. After all, perhaps if she changed her tactics and tried to be friendly towards these people, they might leave her alone and let her get on with her own life in peace. Also the prospective bonfire appealed to her. That was more her scene than theirs, she thought.

Then another idea came to her, as she thought of Farmer Brown's field which was going to be the scene of the barbecue. Farmer Brown had a stall on the roadside at the entrance to his farm and from it he sold a lot of his farm produce to passing motorists. If he could do that why couldn't she? That way she could get rid of all that she didn't actually need, and make some money into the bargain. Money always came in handy in this new world she lived in.

It didn't occur to her for a minute that there was quite a similarity between this and what her cousin was already doing with her mail order catalogues. If it had done she would have run a mile!

The next day she dragged an old table down the drive to the gate, and got Grimpuss to organise some help from a few bats and rats, and between them they all transported a range of vegetables from the shed to the table. A carefully printed notice completed it. 'BUY YOUR VEGETABLES HERE. ALL HOME GROWN'. And Grimolda sat down on a bit of tree trunk to wait for her customers to roll up.

There was one difference that she hadn't taken into account. Her entrance was on a little twisty back road – Farmer Brown's was on a major trunk road. There was another drawback too. The few cars that travelled along her twisty road normally never felt like slowing down. They were more inclined to speed up to get past the gloom as quickly as possible, and the sight of the dingy old lady perched on the tree stump only accelerated their progress.

After three hours of this Grimolda was getting quite fidgety and had started standing up and beckoning to approaching cars, which, to her further annoyance, rather than slowing them down, sped them up even more!

As night fell, a dejected Grimolda trundled all her wares back up the drive. Well, this idea was obviously a non-starter, so there was nothing for it but to fall back on the invitation from the Residents' Association. She got out the circular and read it again. "Please inform us if you're willing to participate," it said, "and someone will visit you to allocate the various duties and to co-ordinate all aspects and eventualities. We would like this first event to be an unmitigated success and will do everything within our power towards that effectuation. Please telephone or write to Evelyn Peabody at the above address and telephone number, explaining in which manner you wish to offer your services. We gratefully anticipate your generosity."

Hmph, thought Grimolda, *what a lot of verbal garbage.* Still, it was the only way she could see to get rid of her veg before they all became a heap of mould in her shed. Although she hated too-fresh vegetables, equally she didn't like them to get too rotten. There was a limit, after all.

Not possessing a phone, there was only one thing to do. She went to look for paper and pen, and, heading the sheet "The Nettles", she wrote in a spidery hand, "I will donate some garden produce for your barbecue," and signed it, "G. Grizz", stuck it in an envelope, addressed it, and went off to post it.

She regretted it the moment it left her hand and vanished into the dark depths of the post box at the foot of the road. She was soon to find out just what she had let herself in for!

Chapter Six

A few days later Grimolda was in the kitchen changing the water in her tank of piranha fish, when her early warning system started sending out frantic messages, meaning there was an intruder around. Her bats were especially sensitive to anything alien. She went into a front room and peered out from behind the curtains.

A very small car stood at the front door, and from it a tall, thin figure was disentangling itself. Grimpuss was sitting on the roof of the car, watching every move with cold calculation.

Having extricated himself with difficulty, the man then approached the front door and lifted the door knocker in such a tentative fashion that when he let it fall the only sound to be heard was a rusty rattle. He made another attempt and this time the noise he achieved made him jump. He stood back and looked at the house in some trepidation and then returned to the door knocker. He obviously wasn't going to go away, so Grimolda shuffled through to the hall and opened the door an inch or two. "Yes?" she grunted.

"Er – um – I'm looking for Mr Grizz," said the young man nervously.

"No Mr Grizz here," retorted Grimolda, and started to close the door.

"Er – is this residence not 'The Nettles?'" said the young man, taking a step forward.

"Well, what if it is?" Grimolda was showing her usual lack of charm in the presence of a mere person.

"I've – um – come on behalf of the Residents' Association. It's about the b-b-b-barbecue," stammered the young man.

She peered at him suspiciously, opening the door another inch or two. "What's your name?"

"Evelyn Peabody," said the young man with an apologetic cough.

"Oh," said the witch, looking him up and down. "I thought you would be a woman. You'd better come in. I wrote you the letter."

"Oh. Jolly good – I mean I'm glad I've come to the correct address. I'm afraid I had surmised from your letter that *you* were a *man*." He coughed nervously and blushed. "Not a very nice day is it? I hope my car isn't in your way," he babbled as he followed Grimolda into the house. She led the way into her front room. It was so long since she had been in it that the dust and cobwebs took her aback. They both stood and looked round idiotically for a minute and then she pushed him into a chair and went to open the curtains wider, but on second thoughts decided that more daylight was inadvisable.

The young man was meanwhile peering into the gloom around him, trying to make out what was actually in the room, to be brought back with a start by Grimolda's grating voice.

"So, what do you want then?"

"Well – er – um – I – er – we're very pleased to know that you are willing to participate – em – Miss – Mrs – er – Madam. What we need to ascertain now is the nature of your donation, and the quantity."

"Obviously," said Grimolda, "*I* first need to know how many people you are expecting."

"Oh – ah – well – yes – I don't really know, but we will verify the number of those expecting to attend once we have sold more tickets."

"Well, that's not much use," snapped Grimolda. "How do I know how much to give you if I don't know how many are going to eat it? At least give me a rough idea."

The young man thought hard. "Perhaps a hundred? Or maybe two hundred, or if people bring along friends as well it could be three hundred?"

"Hmph," said Grimolda. Her opinion of this young man, which had been low to begin with anyway, was descending rapidly to dismal depths.

"Well, I'll expect to supply meat, fish, eggs, and vegetables for two hundred. You can let me know the number of tickets you've sold the day before and I can provide more or less as required."

Mr Peabody's mouth, which had fallen open at this announcement, refused to return to base and he stared at Grimolda for what seemed an age before he at last pulled himself together and started babbling again. "Very good of you – er – Madam. I really – er – we – er – were only expecting small donations from each resident, and I was anticipating having to computate and assimilate the offers to achieve a satisfactory result. But – er – if you supply it all, it will be so much simpler, but, really, we couldn't expect you to do so much – I mean – to provide *all* the food..." He ground to a halt.

"I could give you drink as well," said Grimolda, thinking it would be no bother to make some more gallons of her deadly nightshade wine while she was at it.

"Oh how generous – I really don't know what to say – how to express my thanks – how will we all be able to vouchsafe our eternal gratitude?"

"Well really not at all," said Grimolda, slamming him with her usual flair, "I've got far too much here, and don't know what to do with it. It'll be wasted otherwise."

Mr Peabody was speechless. That this old lady was willing to donate the food for the entire barbecue was overwhelming, but it appeared now that she could actually produce it all from her own premises! From his journey along her drive, hemmed in by a dark, dank wood, he would never have believed this possible. She must have a very large vegetable garden and henhouses and dear knows what else hidden away somewhere.

"Well, well, I think I have all the information required at the moment," he said, rising to go, as the old lady was showing no signs of offering him a cup of tea, and indeed was rather giving him the impression that he was overstaying his welcome, as she was moving steadily nearer the door. He turned to pick up his hat, which he'd laid on the back of the chair, and immediately leapt a foot in the air. An animal was staring at him through the gloom. It looked as if it was about to pounce on him, but, as it didn't move, and as he looked closer, he relaxed and breathed a sigh of relief. It was obviously stuffed!

"How interesting," he said by way of conversation. "Er – what is it?"

"Wild-cat," grunted Grimolda.

Looking around with eyes now accustomed to the gloom, Mr Peabody could see now that the room was full of stuffed animals. He bent and peered at a black furry thing that sat on the table beside his chair. It gave him the shivers. He was glad he hadn't accidentally put his hand on it earlier!

"Bird-eating spider," said Grimolda gruffly, relenting a bit. "One of my favourite pets, but it got out of the house one frosty day and got pneumonia and died. Couldn't part with it so stuffed it."

He looked at her askance, and made a beeline for the door.

"Well, thank you indeed – this visit has been most efficacious," he began to gush and proffered his hand, which Grimolda made no effort to shake. "I will communicate with you again nearer the crucial date," he beamed, and as he tripped down the steps, the door slammed behind him.

Once outside he sagged weakly against his car for a

bit before summoning up enough strength to get in and drive away. He looked around and realised that there was no way that he could turn to drive out. The narrow drive ran straight up to the front door without getting any wider. He had to reverse all the way back to the entrance.

As he came out of the gateway and drove back along the road to Newtown, his spirits soared, and he found he was actually humming to himself. He didn't quite know whether this was due to the material success of his visit or relief at getting away alive and in right mind from the weirdest surroundings he had ever been in. He wasn't aware that Grimpuss had hitched a lift as far as the entrance, and then leapt from the car roof to the gatepost, from which vantage point his gleaming eyes followed the car until it was out of sight.

Chapter Seven

"I'll be glad when I see the last of this barbecue. I knew I'd regret it," grumbled Grimolda to herself, as Grimpuss sneered at her with an 'I told you so' look on his face. It was still a few days away, but Grimolda had been constantly pestered by the ineffectual Mr Peabody, who had for some reason come to rely on her advice, and kept coming back to pick her brains. He seemed totally inept at making decisions, or in fact working anything out in a logical, practical fashion. *I suppose I should be flattered that a human should think so highly of me*, she admitted grudgingly, *and only for my brain power, not for my talents*. Why the residents had chosen him of all people to organise the barbecue in the first place she couldn't make out. But it was the usual story. No-one else could be bothered doing all the work, and it had landed on the shoulders of poor Peabody, who just couldn't say no.

He now left his car just inside the entrance gates when he visited her. He didn't relish the idea of walking the length of the drive, but reversing all the way was worse. He'd now begun to get the feeling that something was accompanying him every time and that he was being constantly watched. Although he tried to shake this feeling off, he just couldn't rid himself of it.

In walking up the drive he was at least in the open, as it were, and could see what was around him, and he was so busy picking his way round the potholes that he wasn't aware that there actually was a dark shadow slinking along behind him or sometimes flitting along above him, and nasty cold eyes taking in every step of his progress.

I really couldn't have done all this organising without the old lady's help, he mused as he made his way up the drive yet again. Not that she had done much more than yet again assemble his scattered thoughts and clarify the whole situation, so that where before everything had been a hopeless jumble, his plan of campaign was now quite orderly. All the ends were being tied up in the right knots and it looked as if there were going to be no hitches at all.

If only the old lady had a phone, he thought, as he nearly sprained his ankle, and, much as he respected her organising ability, he cringed every time he came face to face with her. Of course he could have written to her this time as all he had to do was invite her to light the bonfire and set the whole proceedings off. Everyone on the committee had agreed that such a generous benefactor had to be acknowledged and the best way was to invite her to perform the lighting up ceremony (it had been taken for granted that she was going to be there).

He did feel he should ask her in person. A note seemed too casual and lacking in respect. So here he was trundling his way up the gloomy drive for the umpteenth time, and he had absolutely no idea what came over him when, on reaching the front door, instead of announcing his presence by knocking, he hesitated, then set off at a tangent round the side of the house.

In not one of his visits had Miss Grizz revealed anything about herself or even told him what exactly she was going to provide for the barbecue, what she grew, or where she grew it. Presumably she was going to buy in the meat and the fish – unless she had a trout farm in her wood, and a herd of cattle! And where did she grow her veg?

He had prattled away merrily about his problems and she had straightened him out nicely, but she had given away absolutely nothing about herself. His intense curiosity had finally taken over and now he found himself stealthily creeping round the house to see what wonders the old lady was concealing.

He didn't know what he was expecting, but it was with a sense of disappointment that he discovered that the back of the house was in exactly the same state as the front. The whole place seemed to be hemmed in by closely packed trees. If anything the back was even less prepossessing because, as well as the trees, there were large areas of mangled undergrowth, and the place was overrun with weeds. In fact the house and grounds looked for all the world as if they had been deserted for centuries.

There were one or two excuses for paths leading off into the undergrowth, and he set off down one of them, completely nonplussed but still expecting to find something in the way of a vegetable garden. All that happened was that he was getting deeper and deeper into the woods, which were getting creepier and creepier. Suddenly all hell seemed to break loose. There were whirrings and screechings all around him and dark shapes flew at him from every direction. He turned and fled and promptly tripped over a tree root and fell flat on his face. He lay there quite still for a moment, more from terror than any desire to stay put, and suddenly the disturbance vanished as quickly as it had started. He sat up and tested gently for sprains or breaks, but he seemed to still be in one piece, although his face and hands were now on fire from the nettles he had fallen into, and his clothes were torn by brambly thorns. He could only think that he'd disturbed some roosting birds, but he had no wish to investigate farther.

He retraced his steps as quietly as he could and somehow emerged at a different part of the wood, alongside a shed that he hadn't seen before. The door was locked. He peered through a dirty cobwebby window. It appeared to contain a lot of mouldy-looking stuff that looked as if it was on its way to being compost. There was a nasty smell seeping out between the timbers. He turned away in disgust and bumped right into Grimolda, who had crept up behind him. A guilty flush spread all over his countenance, and he hopped from one foot to the other as the old lady glared at him and snapped, "Well, what are you doing here, snooping about?"

"Oh Miss Grizz, I – I – I wasn't snooping, I assure you – I would never dream of being so devious. I – I couldn't get any answer at the front door so I circumnavigated the house and got slightly lost, I'm afraid."

"Hmph," said Grimolda. "You'd better come in anyway."

She led the way to the back door. As he followed her into the kitchen, Mr Peabody looked around in increasing amazement and consternation. He had believed the front room to be all cobwebby and dusty because the old lady obviously didn't entertain much, if at all, and therefore didn't use that room, but now he found that the whole house appeared to be in the same condition. The kitchen was filthy – and antiquated. There was no cooker, fridge, or washing machine. There was no evidence in fact of there being any electricity in the house! No light switches, no ceiling lights or lamps. The poor old soul must have hardly any money surely, or was she perhaps a miser who hoarded it all? How she came to be donating all this food he just couldn't understand. The only place where cooking could be done appeared to be the old range which crackled and spat at the back of the room.

In a corner a black cat was devouring what had obviously been a very large bird. Bits of wing and bone protruded from its mouth and it eyed him balefully from above the carnage. The big table in the centre of the room was covered in dust. And a plate with unsavoury looking leftovers lay on the floor beside an old rocking chair. There appeared to be little else in the room but a broom leaning against the wall, but from the look of the dirty floor it didn't seem to serve any particular purpose.

He stood there, trying not to come in contact with

anything. Miss Grizz made no move to invite him to sit down. Indeed there was only one chair in the room – the rocking chair.

"Well?" the old lady snapped.

"I've really come with an invitation," stammered Mr Peabody. "We would be so honoured if you would perform the opening ceremony as it were and light the bonfire at our little festivity."

Grimolda was quite taken aback. She had had no intention of going, never mind sticking her neck out. She didn't want to be physically involved with these people.

She started to protest.

"Please. Miss Grizz. Please. We are so beholden to you and we would like to bestow on you a meritorious honour. We were going to invite the Mayoress, and then luckily before we did so, someone – in fact *several* – of the residents put your name forward. You've become quite illustrious don't you know?"

Grimolda was amazed. She had never imagined that donating some food to these people was going to have such far-reaching consequences. It had never occurred to her that her actions would result in their thinking of her as a benefactor and friend! She shrank from this prospect – it was almost as bad as Grimolive's overdose of sweetness – and was about to withdraw all her help, but two things stopped her. One was that they had put her before their Mayoress, which was indeed a feather in her cap, and the other was what they wanted her to do. She really fancied lighting their bonfire.

"Oh all right," she said grudgingly, and Mr Peabody breathed a sigh of relief. He even felt sufficiently emboldened to ask, "By the way – er – er – I was wondering – er – what exactly are you going to provide for the barbecue? You haven't really disclosed the nature of your donation except in the most general terms. I was wondering – er..." His voice tailed off as Grimolda gave him a withering scowl.

"Never mind, young man. You're getting far too nosey for my liking. Send someone up with transport on the morning of the day – that'll be quite soon enough to find out."

As Evelyn Peabody stumbled back down the drive, he began to get a sinking feeling in the pit of his stomach. Had he been wise to accept this old dear's offer in the first place? Was she perhaps slightly unhinged? Did she really intend to give them this food? If so, where was she going to get it all? Perhaps she was living in an imaginary world of her own. Oh dear!

But her beady eyes and sharp talk didn't give any weight to that theory. For the next few days leading up to BB Day, as it was becoming known, he swithered back and forward between premonitions of terrible disaster and the faint hope that she wouldn't let him down. He didn't tell anyone else but carried the whole burden on his poor, thin shoulders, and gave vague answers any time he was questioned. He was a quivering bundle of nerves.

Chapter Eight

Evelyn Peabody awoke in a cold sweat. He was trembling all over. The barbecue had been a total disaster. No food had turned up and when he had gone to 'The Nettles' to investigate, there was no-one there – the old lady had vanished. When he looked in the windows there was nothing inside that he recognised. Even the house looked unfamiliar. He felt as if he had never been there before. He had gone back to Farmer Brown's field and found it in chaos. The bonfire was just a little heap of twigs; the people who were responsible for building it up had obviously shirked that task and everyone was arguing and shouting and the minute they saw him they turned on him like a pack of hyenas, and chased him out of the field and down the road. He had reached his house only in the nick of time to avoid being caught and lynched on the spot. He was still absolutely terrified.

He reached out a trembling hand and turned the clock on his bedside table round to see it better, and then looked at it again. Saturday the tenth, said the date bit. But that was the date of the barbecue. Had his clock stopped?

It took him fully two minutes to come to the realisation that today was truly Saturday the tenth and he had been dreaming and had just had a nightmare. It was all so real; he could still feel the breath of the mob on his neck, and hear the thudding footsteps echoing down the street behind him.

He sagged back against the pillows in weak exhaustion. Knowing that his recent experience was just a bad dream didn't cheer him up at all. It only meant that the whole day was still in front of him, and it could be such a fiasco that his dream might well come true.

That morning seemed to drag interminably. He had never known time to pass so slowly. After he had washed and dressed, and made and eaten his breakfast, he had washed the dishes, then sat down and read his newspaper from end to end and it was still only ten o'clock. Every few minutes he got this urge to dash up to Farmer Brown's field to see what was happening, and it was with great difficulty he restrained himself. After all, he had organised everything and delegated every task to somebody; nothing had been left out, thanks to Miss Grizz's business acumen. Every duty had been listed and duplicated, so that not only did they all know what they were each supposed to do, but they also knew what everyone else was supposed to do, so that it should be an integrated work force, not a lot of individuals running around in their own little orbits unaware of whether their efforts were combining to make a satisfactory whole or not. He didn't need to appear until an hour or so before it was due to start. If anything went very wrong, they would let him know, and in any case he had a feeling that his presence would even be undesirable. There is nothing worse than having someone peering over your shoulder all the time, checking up on you.

He then got a craving to go down town and look at the shops to pass the time but he couldn't do that either. He couldn't leave the house in case something did go wrong and they were trying to contact him. In the end he got out a jigsaw puzzle that he had been given at Christmas, which was perhaps not such a good idea as it didn't occupy his mind at all, only his eyes and hands, so every minute or two he would surrender to another worry, another fear.

By five o'clock he had advanced from being a bundle of nerves, which was at least a whole feeling, to being split into hundreds of little slivers of nerves – not a nice way to be at all. But no-one had phoned and no-one had called. No news was surely good news?

He went upstairs and looked in his wardrobe for some suitably casual clothes. There wasn't much choice, as he only had one casual jacket and one pair of corduroy trousers – he was very much a collar and tie man. However, as he surveyed the result in the mirror he was quite pleased with what he saw. The brown cords looked quite good with the tweed jacket and the brown polo-neck pullover made him look quite the country gent.

Collecting his master list from the hall table, he set off at more of a trot than a walk, in his eagerness to get there and not put it off any longer.

Farmer Brown's field was a scene of bustling activity. Evelyn Peabody stood in the middle of it for a while entirely unnoticed, and he began to feel as if he was not there when someone rushing past called out, "Hi Ev, great weather for it isn't it?"

Two things then clicked. The first was that he had never been called Ev before (and he rather liked that, it had such an air of friendliness about it). Hardly anyone spoke to him by name; it seemed to embarrass people as much as it embarrassed him to be called by what was generally a girl's name. The second was that he hadn't even taken the weather into consideration. It was a lovely evening for November, quite mild really. There was a tiny little breeze wafting about that seemed to freshen everything up and provided a welcome relief for the workers. Three large squares of turf had been cut and rolled away to a corner so that the field could be returned to normal afterwards, and two big barbecues had been built on bricks and grids on the clearings and the charcoal was beginning to glow in readiness. At the side of each barbecue a smaller fire was getting going under a large metal sheet. This had been one of Miss Grizz's brainwaves. As food was cooked it was to be transferred to these to keep warm (there was nothing that Grimolda disliked more than cold food that was meant to be hot). On the third bit of bare ground another fire was heating up the soup and cooking the vegetables in pots suspended from a strong rod, in its turn suspended on a sort of scaffolding.

Near all this were trestle tables, laden with paper plates, cups, plastic cutlery and napkins. Women were busy cutting up hunks of French bread. Nearer the gate stood a table with an array of glasses, and flagons of dark red wine. Behind that a boy had just poured into a basin some water from a pan bubbling away on a primus stove, and was proceeding to wash a tray of glasses, and as Evelyn watched someone came over and deposited three more glasses on the tray.

Now he knew why everyone was so animated! They had all been sampling the wine. "Hi Ev," came a voice from behind him and the man who had hailed him before appeared with a cardboard box full of glasses and proceeded to line them up on the table.

"Have you had some of this wine yet? It's really something. Go on," and he handed him a beer mug full. He took a tentative sip. It really was delicious.

"Fruity little number, plenty of body eh, Ev?" grinned the man. "It's not just plonk. Real quality there, and there's gallons of it!" And sure enough, under the table were more flagons, all full of the same dark red wine.

Suddenly Evelyn's spirits soared, and a feeling of supreme bliss spread through him. He wandered about among the happy activity with a silly grin on his face and feeling as if his feet were inches off the ground.

People with young children started to drift in. There was to be hot food available from the start so that the kiddies could have something to eat and see the bonfire lit without being kept up too late. Later there was to be music from a group which had donated its services, and the food and drink would hopefully last out till the finish.

In no time the field was filled with laughter and happy chatter, and food was being constantly conveyed from barbecue to paper plates, to the insides of the crowd, and glasses constantly refilled.

"What a success, Ev!"

"Great night, Ev!"

"Super, Ev!" Everywhere he went he was being congratulated and patted on the back and being called Ev, and he found himself stammering with pleasure instead of nerves. "W – w –well really it's not me you've to thank, it's Miss Grizz. It's all her doing."

He was being carried along on such a feeling of euphoria that he didn't even feel hungry. A cup of soup which, even though it was a vivid shade of green, was delicious – he wondered if it was spinach – and bottomless glasses of the rich red wine, seemed to fill him up completely. Surprising since he'd had nothing since breakfast.

Funny, he thought now, how could he have possibly imagined that things could go wrong?

"Hey Ev," said someone, "I've been sent to ask you – where's the old lady who's going to light the bonfire? It's after eight."

Yes indeed. Where was Miss Grizz? Although she had hardly been out of his thoughts, it hadn't occurred to him that she was conspicuous by her absence. He hadn't seen the old soul anywhere. He suddenly felt guilty and started frantically searching the crowd for signs of her. Surely she must be somewhere? But there was no sign of her.

"You did tell her what time the bonfire's to be lit?" asked the man with the matches and the big torch that was to get it all going.

"Yes I think so. I'm sure I did," said Ev in a panic.

What were they to do? The band was standing there waiting to play a fanfare and the photographer from the local newspaper was waiting to get a photograph. Not that any of them seemed bothered – they were all having too good a time; in fact the photographer was holding his camera upside down, and the group seemed unsure of how to hold their instruments. The minutes ticked on. The group started playing Yellow Submarine, doing a balancing act on each other's shoulders. The children were dancing round the unlit bonfire, chanting, "London's not burning, the bonfire's not burning," when suddenly there was Grimolda standing beside him. One minute she wasn't there, the next minute she was. It was as if she'd appeared by magic out of thin air.

"Oh Miss Grizz," he gasped, "I'm so glad you're here. I – I – I've been quite worried, I–"

"Well I am here – what have I to do?"

As the old lady bestowed on him one of her acid glances he stopped gabbling and led her over to the bonfire. At sight of her the children stopped dancing and drew back, the group returned to normal, the cameraman accidentally let off his flash gun, and the man with the torch seemed transfixed to the spot. *Usual reaction*, she thought. She'd even made an attempt to look acceptable, had put on a clean cloak and combed her hair.

I'll show them, she thought, and grabbing the torch from the man that held it, she raised it high above her head and hurled it onto the top of the pile. Immediately the whole bonfire lit up and blazed and coloured sparks flew into the sky, lighting it up vividly. The entire crowd stood transfixed to the spot. There was a whisper behind Ev. "Someone must have put fireworks on the bonfire. Is that not dangerous? But doesn't it look fantastic?"

All of a sudden the scene came to life again, the band struck up, the cameraman snapped away, the crowd cheered and started singing, and the man with the matches looked in puzzlement at the unopened box still in his hand. And the bonfire banged and plopped and fizzed and whistled and flared and changed colour every second. And Ev found he was holding Miss Grizz's hand, while she had a look of disgust on her face, which didn't in the slightest stop him from saying, "Oh Miss Grizz, this has all been wonderful! The whole thing! I just don't know what to say – I can't thank you enough. You've done it all, you know." He'd even forgotten to use his usual big words.

"Yes I know," started Grimolda acidly, and then pride at what she had achieved made her say something which took her completely by surprise. "I'm glad it's been such a success," she said, and vanished as quickly as she'd arrived.

Everyone promptly forgot the strange old lady and proceeded to enjoy the rest of the evening as if there was no tomorrow.

It was only when he was helping to clear up the debris the next day that Ev asked one of the women what the rest of the food had been like.

"Well," she said, "We were a bit put off at first when it arrived. The poor old dear is obviously into French cuisine, but instead of frogs' legs she sent us whole frogs! Joan and Ethel had an awful job cutting off all the legs – they felt quite sick – but I must say I've never tasted anything so delicious in my life once they were cooked. I never thought to see the day when I'd enjoy frogs' legs! And then there was caviar with raw eggs and garlic. I was all for cooking the eggs, but someone said to separate them and eat the yolks with the caviar. We had it on the French bread and it was lovely. And we made sort of spinachy omelettes with the whites and some of the veg. And then there were sausages that must have been homemade by someone – I don't know where the old lady got hold of them but they were really delicious – a funny colour for sausages, but they can look like anything nowadays can't they! And the fish was so tasty too – I don't know what it was – probably French again, and the vegetables were lovely. It was all a real treat and Bill said to me after, he said, 'Let's go to France for our holidays next year,' and you know he's never wanted to go abroad. It really was great, Ev. How kind of the old lady. She must be loaded. Is she, Ev?"

"I don't know about that," said Ev. "She lives very simply really."

At that moment Grimolda was sitting in her rocking chair cackling away to herself, in delight really, at the way she and only she had been responsible for all suburbia having a good time – all those people who used to sign petitions and send complaints, and children who used to make faces at her and shout rude names. All, absolutely all of them, had had the time of their lives – all thanks to her.

They even seemed to like the same food that she

did. The nettle soup, the stinkfish from the stagnant pond in her wood, the snake's eggs, the frogs and the frogspawn, the sausages made of a mixture of minced ferret, mouldy bread and snake's blood, the mixed veg, a combination of creeping cucumber, spotted cabbage, squashy purple tomatoes and garlic, and her wine.

Or did they enjoy it all because she'd mixed up a pinch of each ingredient in a pot of garlic and snake venom, simmered it in some of her deadly nightshade wine, before she'd left, and cast a spell on it to make it all go down a treat? After all, she didn't want to go down in history as a spoiler of barbecues and bonfires!

She took another sip of her wine and creakily rocked back and forward in her creaky rocking chair, cackling and creaking, creaking and cackling.

Grimpuss just couldn't understand why she was enjoying herself so much.

Chapter Nine

Grimpuss had been getting more and more fed up. While his mistress had been sorting out vegetables, gathering ingredients and making sausages, collecting frogs and storing them in her larder, brewing up her own brand of wine, and performing all the other tasks that were involved with the barbecue, he had been totally neglected. He was used to wandering about doing his own thing, but he was also used to getting a welcome on his return and a bit of praise if he came back with an extra large 'bag' of birds after a day's hunting. Grimolda was normally around at some point to share his little pleasures or at least speak to him. To be honest he was still smarting from the stupendous row she'd given him at Grimolive's, and it had been slowly mouldering away inside him, fired progressively by all the inattention.

Anyway, for a while he had got a little satisfaction from going around the neighbourhood during the day and wreaking quiet havoc wherever he took the notion.

It all came to a head one day when, from a tall tree in Grimolda's domain, he observed a particularly insipid and sweet little cat that lived in one of the houses on the other side of the boundary wall. He had often watched her antics from his tall tree, and all the oohs and aahs of love and affection ladled on her by her doting mistress, and his little malevolent eyes had taken in the movements of the household while his little malevolent mind planned and schemed.

So one day when the cat was sitting on her garden wall with her eyes shut, soaking in a bit of wintry sunshine, and her owners had left for the supermarket in their car, he quietly slipped into their house by an upstairs window and proceeded to rearrange the interior more to his liking. He tore up a negligee that was lying on the bed, knocked all the bottles off the dressing table, then went downstairs, where he found some knitting and balls of wool on the settee, and took great delight in pushing and pulling them about and whirling them round his head until they were a lovely tangled mess. He knew who would immediately get the blame for that – exactly what he wanted. Having started the proceedings in a most satisfactory fashion, he then looked round to see what other havoc he could wreak. A collection of glass animals along the top of the bookcase was very inviting, and he did a little ballet dance along there, pitting and patting the ornaments into the air as if they were tennis balls.

A few clawing runs up and down the curtains left their mark nicely, and a splash into a bowl of custard in the kitchen resulted in a gooey mess and a nice trail of paw prints all over the surfaces, including the carpet in the dining room. In passing, he knocked a pot half full of cooling coffee off the table, which made a lovely spreading stain on the carpet. He was having such a fantastic time that he got quite carried away. He was in the middle of tearing the net screens on the kitchen window when all of a sudden, "What the-?" came from the doorway into the hall, and there were the owners returned from their shopping! Grimpuss had lost all sense of time! He stood frozen to the spot while the couple advanced, uttering a barrage of expletives. The husband lifted a carving knife from the work top, which suddenly galvanised Grimpuss into action and he flew past them and out of the front door, which luckily was open as the couple hadn't even started unloading the car when they'd heard strange sounds issuing from the house.

Grimpuss fled back to his own territory in a roundabout way – he didn't want them to know where he'd come from – passing on his way the insipid little cat who was stretching herself luxuriously after her nap.

From the safety and camouflage of his tall tree he watched and listened to the goings on as the couple found every bit of his handiwork, getting louder and more irate the more they discovered. It was all small consolation for the pleasure he would have had seeing that silly little cat being blamed if things had gone as planned. He was a very disgruntled Grimpuss, and every bit as fed up as before.

After that things went back to normal for a while, and Grimolda was more like her old self, apart from occasional absent-mindedness, for example forgetting to give him his evening treat of roasted newts before she went to bed. But somehow he was still feeling restless. One evening he was sitting there in the kitchen listening to Grimolda's snores and snuffles, and staring into space really, but the space happened to materialise into her broomstick standing against the wall at the back door. An idea started to formulate.

Aha! he thought, or rather, *Miaowha!* and he slunk over to the broomstick, gave it a nasty little biff which knocked it over, leapt at the latch, which got the door open, and, dragging the broomstick outside, he looked at it for a moment, savouring his anticipation before he finally leapt on it and took off. The annoyance and anxiety he had experienced on his previous encounter with it didn't seem to register and he soared away into the night sky with an overwhelming feeling of being Master of the Universe.

Initially he just flitted around aimlessly, enjoying the absolute freedom, and returning quite quickly. He took to going off on these joyrides every night, always making sure that he arrived home long before his mistress awoke, as half the fun was the fact that she had absolutely no idea what he was up to.

He felt drunk with power and as dizzy as a kid on a rollercoaster. Of course he wasn't just flying around sedately, but doing cartwheels, looping the loop, whizzing up and diving down like a bomber pilot. It was on one of these flips that he came in contact with reality again as he came so close to a rooftop that he nearly came a cropper. He was only a whisker away from disaster as he zoomed past the offending roof, narrowly missing a cat that had been sitting on the roof minding its own business, and terrifying other cats out on the prowl down below. Their petrified yowling wakened the whole neighbourhood and set people opening windows and shouting abuse and hurling shoes at shadows.

Which brought him back to earth as it were, and he started doing things on a simpler scale. Like choosing a house at random and going down its chimney and pattering black sooty paw prints all over the carpet before returning the way he had come. He had problems with houses that didn't have open fires but gas ones and/or blocked chimneys. If washing was left out overnight, he pulled it all off the line and tossed it about all over the place.

All this provided him with endless entertainment and so much exercise and excitement that he stayed home most days and slept! Grimolda was too busy to notice or she might have thought he was ill. And then, when the barbecue was becoming history, disaster struck.

After visiting four houses in succession, and being stopped short by boarded up fireplaces which presumably had gas fires, he decided to head for the open country, where there were likely to be coal or log fires, and unblocked chimneys.

He was swooping about, changing direction at random, when he discovered he was over a wood which was turning into a forest with just a track running through it. He was about to turn back when he saw smoke curling up from among the trees.

Hooray, he thought and dived down. The vague outline of a house loomed up at the end of the track. It was all in darkness – well it would be – it was now about 3 a.m. Grimpuss didn't stop to wonder why there was so much smoke pouring out of the chimney at this hour, but leaving the broomstick propped against the chimney stack, he shot down one of the other three non-smoking chimneys, and came out into what appeared to be a dining room. It was heavily shuttered and sparsely furnished, with only a table and chairs in the middle of the room. In the darkness he could just make out an array of bottles on the table. But there was a nice thick piled carpet on the floor, and he proceeded to dance a jig over it and roll about a bit as well.

Suddenly he heard footsteps and a voice on the other side of the door. It said, "I'll get another bottle," and then the door opened and the light clicked on. There stood Grimpuss, caught in an extravagant attitude, like in a game of statues, in a circle of black sooty splodges. For a moment he was frozen to the spot, but only momentarily. There seemed to be only one course of action open to him, and he tore past the man who appeared to be struck dumb and was standing with his mouth open. Grimpuss flew down the corridor and through the only other open door.

A group of men were sitting round a table in a large dimly lit kitchen, studying closely a pile of papers in front of them, and listening earnestly to a large man who was pointing out something on what appeared to be a map. That is they had been, but when Grimpuss tore in they all rose in consternation and started shouting at each other and him. Chaos reigned as he dashed about and they dashed about after him, tripping over themselves and each other. There was no escape route here, as this was the room with the blazing fire.

Why he hadn't gone up his first chimney he didn't know, and he turned and headed for it now, but, as he scrambled into the corridor again, the man with the bottle was blocking the entrance to that room, so Grimp spun round and headed the other way and some stairs came into view. Up he flew, and through an open doorway halfway along the landing. But... no fireplace, and a window that was heavily shuttered, and also – the room was occupied – by two figures huddled in a corner – but they appeared to be helpless, being bound and gagged. At that point another man stepped out from behind the door. He had a gun in his hand and a startled expression on his face. Grimpuss didn't stop to investigate further but dashed back out and down the stairs, followed by the man with the gun. As he came back down the bottom turn, another door opened and a blast of cold air ushered in another man, also armed with a gun.

"What's up? What's going on here?" he shouted. Grimpuss, poised on the bottom step, could see the hall filling up with the men from the kitchen and, to his left, the big man who was pointing at him.

The man with the gun was blocking the door to the outside, but Grimpuss could see no alternative but to dive between the man's legs and out to freedom, but the man was quicker and caught him by the tail and pulled him back. Grimpuss, terrified, flailed about and hit out with claws and teeth. As they contacted flesh and scraped down his face, the man screamed and let go and Grimpuss leapt through the door.

"I'll show him!!" shouted the man, now quite enraged, and he set off in pursuit, firing his gun in all directions.

"Come back and shut up!" shouted the big man, running after him, and all the other men tumbled out of the house and joined in.

Everywhere Grimp went the way was blocked, and the gunman was close on his heels the whole time, still firing wildly.

Trying not to get in the line of fire, Grimpuss sped on, twisting and turning and darting about, until he landed on a path which seemed to be leading deeper into the forest. He put on a spurt when suddenly a large shape loomed up in front of him; a boot came out and kicked him with very good aim through an open door into darkness. The door banged shut and a key turned in the lock.

"Got you!" said a voice, and footsteps moved away.

Grimp was limp! He'd just had the fright of his life. Nothing like this had ever happened to him before, and he was cornered with no way out. He was locked in a strongly built hut with no windows, no air vents, no chimneys – no escape. He was a prisoner.

Chapter Ten

Grimpuss was shivering, not only from the cold but from fear – he couldn't remember ever feeling like this. He was terrified. He didn't know how long he crouched like this, surrounded by a black silence, when suddenly it was broken by an ear-piercing sound and the cracks between the door and lintel lit up with flashing lights. Grimpuss leapt for the rafters and clung there, petrified.

He now identified the sound as police sirens, which did nothing to dispel his terror. Added to all that came shouts and yells and the *rat-a-tat* of gunfire. There seemed to be a running battle going on around him. He clung to his rafter and curled up as small as he could. Bullets could travel through wood, couldn't they?

The shots and the shouts gradually became more spaced out until they dwindled away to a solitary bang and then nothing. Black silence again – well, slightly grey – there was obviously a bright light still shining somewhere.

The silence stretched out and Grimpuss was just thinking about coming down from his perch when a voice piped up from the other side of the door. The key turned in the lock, the door opened, a torch flashed about briefly and a voice in the darkness behind the torch said, "Don't know why it was locked – there's nothing here," and before Grimpuss could twitch a whisker the door was shut and locked again.

"Better," said the same voice. "Forensic might find something. There's obviously been someone shut up here at some point."

Yes, ME, and I'm still here! Grimpuss screamed silently. But he was afraid of the police and didn't dare draw their attention to him.

There was the sound of a match being struck and a second voice said, "Wasn't it lucky though that Jim took a notion to come down that side road when he came off duty and heard the shots and radioed for back-up. We've been looking for that gang for years. I wonder what made them make such a racket? Overconfidence probably and thinking there was no-one around to hear them. Just shows you."

"Well, lucky for us anyway," said the first voice, "and for the poor couple they had taken prisoner in their own house." The voices and footsteps faded away into silence. Then there was the sound of motors starting up in the distance and the faint grey light disappeared, and Grimpuss was left again in silence and darkness in his prison.

Why he hadn't miaowed and told the police of his presence he didn't know, apart from the fact that he had a dread of anyone in uniform, and the police were high on his list, even though he'd never actually come in contact with them. They would probably have said, "Nice kitty, poor thing, why would anyone lock it up?" and not done anything more than let him out if he had purred at them.

Anyway his brainpower didn't stretch to a course of action that wasn't immediately obvious, and it would have never occurred to him to pretend to be a nice little cat. One thing that could be said for him – he had no deceit in him, he was just quite straightforwardly nasty!

Meanwhile, back at 'The Nettles', Grimolda got up as usual as dawn broke, poked up the cinders of her fire to get it going again, made her usual breakfast of a sort of mash of furry fungus and squashy tomatoes thickened with oatmeal, brewed up a pot of her usual dandelion tea, and settled down to enjoy it. She did look about at one point for Grimpuss, and came to the conclusion that he must have been up and out before her.

It wasn't until evening and there was still no sign of the cat that she began to wonder where he was, but again she wasn't worried, and left out an extra big plateful of roasted newts for him. He was maybe out on a long and fruitless hunt and she could imagine what kind of effect that would have on him. He would need cheering up when he got back.

It wasn't until morning and there was still no sign of the cat, and the plate of roasted newts was still intact, that she began to get really worried. No amount of calling had any result. It began to get through to her that he might have been missing for over 24 hours. And then she found that not only Grimpuss was missing – her broomstick was gone!

Well that made it simpler. Or did it? The only place she could think of that he would be likely to go to on the broomstick was Grimolive's. But why would he want to go there, of all places? She remembered seeing a telephone in Grimolive's hall, so that was at least a way of checking up and easing her worried mind. She stalwartly marched down the drive, out of the gate and along the road to the nearest phone box. Not knowing the first thing about phones and phone boxes was a slight drawback as a) she didn't know how to use it, and b) she hadn't brought any money. Of course she should have realised that nothing could function without money in this outside world, so there was a bit of delay while she went back to the house for cash. Then she had to find out Grimolive's number, but once her sharp brain grasped the essentials she was away to a flying start, and soon there was Grimolive's voice at the other end of the line, sounding thin and crackly but losing none of its new sugary sweetness.

"Oh Mouldy dear, how nice to hear from you. How are you dear?" she squeaked.

Grimolda, not feeling so obliged to be as polite on the phone as she might be to her cousin in person, killed the small talk and came straight to the point.

"Grimpuss dear? Oh no, I haven't seen him since he left with you," said Grimolive with a shudder, remembering how nasty the cat had been to her, but her kind self won through and she said, "but I'll go and call him just in case." And Grimolda kept putting in more money as the machine gobbled it up, and fumed with impatience not because of the time her cousin was taking but at all the money that was disappearing. Eventually the sweet voice broke into the crackle. "I'm terribly sorry, Mouldy dear, I'm afraid there's no sign of him and Grimy hasn't seen him either."

"Thanks," said Mouldy briefly and put the phone down, leaving Grimolive looking at the receiver in dismay. Her cousin was, if anything, getting more peculiar than ever!

Grimolda, having her simple solution snatched out of her grasp, was now nothing short of frantic. She began to realise how neglectful she had been of late, and how she'd hardly taken any notice of her cat apart from the fact that he had been around.

"He's run away, that's what," she muttered to herself as she marched back up the drive. "How on earth am I going to find him? He could be anywhere! Especially with the broomstick."

The broomstick! She'd forgotten about the broomstick! There might be just a slight chance – she hurried back into the house and, going over to where the broomstick normally stood, she bent down and examined the floor carefully. She then went and got a small shovel and shovelled up, along with the dust from the floor, a few splinters and twigs, which had obviously broken off the broom while it was being moved back and forward.

These she took over to the table and put in a tin bowl. She then magnetised some iron filings and tipped them in. To that lot she added the olfactory ducts from a bloodhound, and some other ingredients from an assortment of bottles which were kept in her kitchen cupboard. Finally she minced up a few of Grimpuss's hairs (of which there were plenty lying around) and sprinkled them on top of the concoction, mixed the whole lot thoroughly, and put it into a long glass jar which fanned out at the top to a trumpet shape.

She sat and looked at it for a bit, then she picked it up and went outside. Although the bats and rats and other pets had seen no sign of him, she couldn't dismiss the fact that Grimpuss might be somewhere near at hand, but hurt and unable to move. So she trailed around for a bit, staring closely at her glass phial, but he was obviously nowhere in the vicinity.

She now had in her hand the wherewithal of finding him – that was to say if he was still attached to the broomstick – but her next problem was how and where to look for him. She herself was pretty helpless without her broomstick. It had never occurred to her that a spare one might be useful; in all the years that she had flitted around, she'd only ever needed the one!

She couldn't go walking round the whole countryside – it would take her months if she went in the wrong direction. She knew what she needed, but the problem was – how to get it? The most sensible thing to do seemed to be to ask her new friend, Mr Peabody. If he couldn't help, which she doubted, he might be able to suggest something.

So back to the phone box went Grimolda, this time prepared for all eventualities, but, when she dialled Ev's number, there was no reply. It hadn't occurred to her that he might be at work. So she set off to look for his house, as she had no idea where he worked.

At six o'clock that evening Ev came down the road to find a strange sight at his front door – Grimolda sitting on the doorstep, looking cold and fretful. Any time he saw her he didn't know whether to be happy or sad. However he really did think of her as a friend after the barbecue, so he stepped forward with outstretched hands.

"Miss Grizz, how nice to see you, and what has brought you here? Do come in. Have you been waiting long? Ooh what cold hands!" He led the way in, babbling away. Although he had discarded big words, he couldn't do anything about his nervousness.

Grimolda was frankly curious about Mr Peabody's house. She'd never been in anyone's house other than poor Grimolive's, so she was pleasantly surprised at Ev's. It was certainly too bright and white and spick and span but there were no horrible sweet colours to offend her eye. In fact everything was very black, white, and grey, so two thirds of it were to be commended. His room seemed to be mainly taken up with a computer and its trappings. Grimolda felt she was quite knowledgeable about these things as a result of her dealings with technology when she bought her television set. If she hadn't been on a serious mission she would have liked to have a go, but she really had to concentrate on her lost cat. She couldn't very well tell him that the cat had gone off on her broomstick! But she did say she had no idea where he was – he could be anywhere.

"And so," she said, "I've come to the conclusion that what I need is a plane!"

Chapter Eleven

Ev was struck dumb, but eventually he managed to stutter, "P-p-p-plane?!" Well that was certainly different – to go looking for a lost cat in a *plane!*

But she was so deadly serious and seemed so sure she would find Grimpuss this way that he thought he'd better humour her and, amazingly, it was actually possible.

"The firm I work for has a helicopter," he said. "They ferry the directors up and down the country to meetings. I don't know whether I could arrange it, but I could try. They sometimes hire it out when they're not using it."

Grimolda's face lit up with delight. *Why*, thought Ev, *she looks quite nice when she smiles!*

"I'll certainly do my best," he said. "I'll give you my phone number at work and you just phone me any time in the morning. Give me an hour or so first to give me time to see what I can do. Now would you like a cup of tea before you go?"

Grimolda was about to say no, but there was beginning to be a sort of rapport between her and Ev, so to her surprise she found herself saying yes.

"It's not everybody's taste, I'm afraid," he said apologetically as he brought the tray through. "I got it at a friend's and I liked it so much I've used it ever since. It's called gunpowder."

And to her surprise Grimolda found that she did like it! And the little hard nutty biscuits were nice too. She couldn't believe that she could actually enjoy food of this kind. And that Ev was going to solve her problem for her was just great. For she had absolutely no doubt that she would find Grimpuss now.

She went away as pleased as Punch, if a witch can be?! As Ev waved goodbye to her and she trotted off, his neighbour appeared from across the street. "Who on earth was that, Ev?" he said, "I nearly chased her away when I saw her sitting on your doorstep for hours – she looked like an old tramp. I'm so glad I didn't. I didn't realise you knew her," and he gave Ev a funny look.

"Oh that's Miss Grizz," said Ev, hunting for an appropriate explanation. "She is – em – rather eccentric."

"You can say that again," said his neighbour.

The helicopter pilot couldn't believe his eyes when he saw his prospective passenger. He had had unusual ones before – they were mostly turbaned sheiks and distinguished-looking foreigners, but this old trampy woman was something else.

He looked at Ev, who had brought her, for some explanation, but when Ev said, "She's lost her cat, Bert," he began to think he was having hallucinations. But who was he to question what sort of people he took up in his helicopter? He was only the pilot and if she had hired it – well, she had hired it. So he helped her up, along with a brown paper parcel, which was very smelly, and an odd-shaped paper bag which she carried very carefully and wouldn't put down.

And off they went.

"Where exactly did you lose your cat?" asked the pilot.

"I've no idea," said Grimolda.

"I mean, presumably he was at home before he got lost, so he'll be around there somewhere?"

"He'll be *miles* from there. Did you think I'd hire a helicopter to look for a cat if he was on my doorstep?" snapped Grimolda.

"Er, no, no, of course not." She did have a point there.

"But you might as well start here and fly round in bigger circles in order to cover as much ground as possible. But I'm positive he's miles away, so it will take some time."

Funny cat, thought Bert, *wandering miles away.* Out loud he said, "D'you think maybe he's been picked up by someone and taken away in their car? That sometimes happens."

"Highly unlikely," snorted Grimolda. Even she

knew that Grimp was the last cat anyone would want to steal.

How the old dear would be able to see her cat from up there Bert couldn't understand, unless it was tartan or fluorescent or something! The old dear wasn't even bothering to look. She was obviously convinced that her cat was really miles away. She just kept looking in her funny-shaped bag. *Maybe one of the cat's toys,* thought the pilot curiously. *She's maybe into Ouija, and thinks she'll find him by association?*

On they went round and round in ever-increasing circles. Bert was quite enjoying himself. It was a beautiful day for November, and he seldom had a chance to enjoy the local scenery. He was more often than not haring up and down the country on tight time schedules.

They settled into a peaceful silence. Grimolda was of course just being unsociable as usual, but Bert didn't know that, and he was quite happy. Below them rivers, meadows, villages floated past. It was as if they were sitting in a little time capsule, quite static, while the world went round and round beneath them like a spinning top. Apart from the fact that the little time capsule was very draughty and noisy, it was quite a pleasant sensation. Grimolda began to compare it favourably with travel by broomstick.

As they went farther, the circling feeling vanished, they just seemed to be covering endless miles of countryside and Bert was wondering how much more of this it would take before the old lady gave up, when, "He's down there!" she cried, pointing. Below them was a vast forest, stretching for miles. She looked in her bag again. Yes, the mixture in the glass phial was glowing faintly.

Bert raised his eyebrows, and followed her pointing finger. "Down there," he gasped incredulously. "You can't see him down there surely, in amongst all that?!"

"Of course I can't see him, but he's there all right – you take my word for it, young man, and take me down there."

Bert was at least relieved that she didn't think she could actually see the cat, otherwise he would really have doubted her sanity. It would take very powerful binoculars indeed to see an animal that size! All he could see apart from trees was the roof of a house which was completely hemmed in by the forest.

"I'm afraid I can't take you down there, we need a clear space to land and there isn't any, but if I follow that road in the distance, we might find a clearing." A mile or two farther on they saw a layby with a clearing beside it with recently felled trees stacked at its side.

"That should be O.K.," he said. "Must be going to make a picnic area there. Suits us fine." And down they went.

Grimolda wasted no time clambering out, but when Bert made to follow she snapped, "Just you wait with the plane. I don't need you."

"But you might get lost," stammered Bert, amazed that she wasn't afraid of going off into this jungle on her own.

"Never," said Grimolda. She appeared to be laughing.

Oh dear, thought Bert, *I can see me losing her and having to go for a search party. I wonder if I should have refused to take her in the first place.* But it was too late now, and he watched with misgivings the purposeful back of the old lady as she strode away down the road with amazing verve for one so aged.

Grimolda was glad to be free of the cage-like helicopter. It did after all have disadvantages. On her broomstick she could have landed exactly where she wanted.

What she hadn't told Bert was that, although she hadn't seen Grimpuss, she *had* seen what looked very much like a broomstick on the roof of the house, and anyway, her phial was not only glowing now, it was quite lit up and beginning to hum the nearer she got to the house.

As she went up the track that led to it she thought the quickest way would be to call him, so she shouted out as loud as she could, "Grimpuss, Grimpuss!"

A policeman, who had been sitting in his car near the house, jumped out of his skin at the eldritch screech, and Grimolda jumped behind a tree just in time, as she rounded a bend in the path and saw him.

He got out of the car and looked around. Had he imagined it? Had he fallen asleep and dreamt it? Then there was a faint miaow from somewhere in the distance. Relieved, he got back in his car. Must have been a wild cat whose yowl had become magnified in his dreamy state.

Grimolda disappeared into the forest to work her way round unseen to the source of the sound. She was delighted at the efficiency of her concoction. Her powers weren't dwindling with disuse after all.

As her paper bag changed from humming to

whistling she risked a stage whisper. "Grimp, where are you?" and another pathetic miaow came from quite near at hand. She soon found the locked door and opened it. Into the sunlight, blinking, came a very poor excuse for a Grimpuss. Grimolda unwrapped her other parcel, and put down in front of him a big helping of roasted newts. She knew that whatever state or mood he was in, that would revive him instantly, and it did.

She was so pleased to have him back she couldn't have cared less what had actually happened to him, and she could see from how pleased he was to see her that he couldn't really have run away. "Just get me down my broomstick," she said, "and mind, there's a policeman guarding the house," the cat jumped, "and we'll be off home."

What has *he been up to?* she wondered. *But I'll find out later. Plenty of time.* And she threw away her scenting powder into the wood. There was a small explosion and some coloured sparks. The policeman jumped again. "This place is having a very bad effect on me," he muttered to himself. "Shouldn't be here on me own."

Grimolda was all set to fly off home with Grimp safely ensconced in front of her when she suddenly remembered Bert and the helicopter. She would have to go back with him of course. Besides she had still to pay for the hire. She couldn't do anything that would let Ev down.

Bert was quite flabbergasted when he saw not only Grimolda but also a black cat coming up the road. He couldn't believe his eyes. "You've actually found your cat?!" he spluttered.

"Of course. I told you he was here," snapped Grimolda, and she and Grimpuss leapt agilely into the helicopter, along with what looked like a mouldy old broom. He looked at it then at Grimolda enquiringly. "Found it along there," she said, "thought it might come in useful." She was getting quite used to this cover-up talk. She seemed to be accepted as a cranky old woman, so why shouldn't she let them keep thinking that's all she was? It was obviously sometimes more useful to be a witch 'out of cloth', she was finding. Like a wolf in sheep's clothing, she chortled to herself. But she would really have to obtain a spare broomstick. She couldn't go through all that again.

She sat back with a sigh. Grimpuss, purring, curled up in her lap. And Bert breathed a sigh of relief as with a whirr and a *whish* they took off for home.

Chapter Twelve

The wedding invitation took Grimolda completely by surprise. She blinked and looked again, scarcely daring to believe her own eyes, but there it was, as large as life, in elaborate gold letters on a cream ground.

OLIVE GRIZZ AND ARTHUR BOYLE
REQUEST THE PLEASURE
OF YOUR COMPANY
AT THEIR FORTHCOMING MARRIAGE
ON SATURDAY THE 13TH DECEMBER
AT HEMINGWAY REGISTRY OFFICE
AT 3 P.M.
AND AFTERWARDS
AT THE GEORGE AND DRAGON,
HEMINGWAY.

Well, really!! Grimolive had done it this time!! Not only had she flipped her lid, when she had started mixing with people and working for them and living among them, but she was actually going to marry one now! Grimolda had never heard the like! She might have understood better if Arthur had been of suitable character, with hidden depths of some kind, a sharp intelligence with perhaps a bit of menace thrown in, but from her brief meeting with him she had soon sized him up as being no more than the chubby, short-sighted, quite harmless, simple soul that his appearance indicated. No hidden depths there. In fact he was probably responsible for Grimolive's transition to sweetness and light.

But the point was, thought Grimolda, was she herself able to, and *would* she, do anything about it? And if she didn't, would she go to the wedding? Something in the corner of the card caught her attention. 'P.T.O.', it said. She turned it over and read, in Grimolive's now flowery handwriting: "Dearest Mouldy, please come, and we would love if you would bring a friend with you. It will be quite a small party really, so the more the merrier. Love, Olive."

"Huh!" snorted Grimolda. Olive, as she now called herself − a bit of conceit that − would be lucky to have her at the wedding, never mind bringing someone else. At that point the last thing she wanted was to be subjected to Grimolive's lifestyle for however short a time. But as the days passed and Grimolda went on with her normal routine, she found herself thinking about this wedding more and more. She was frankly curious. And after all she wouldn't be anywhere near Grimolive's ghastly house. The registry office and the pub should be reasonable enough, and she could perhaps take Ev with her. He would keep her straight. She went down to the cellar, where she had recently had a telephone installed. The telephone people hadn't been able to understand why she wanted it down in the cellar, but, truth to tell, she was a little ashamed of the moment of weakness that had led her to order it, and anyway she didn't want it grinning up at her invitingly every time she walked past it. Far too extravagant it was, so the cellar was the best place for it.

She sat down on a cask of elderberry wine, part of the store that her grandfather had collected many moons ago, and dialled Ev's number.

Of course he would come! Ev was only too delighted.

"It's a hundred miles away. We'll have to go by bus or train," said Grimolda, giving a silent cackle as she imagined his reaction if she'd suggested going by broomstick!

"That's quite all right. We'll go in my car," said Ev. "I know you haven't got transport and I'll be happy to drive you. That's settled then."

Grimolda felt quite cheerful as she put the phone down. She could do with a bit of excitement. Since the barbecue and then the Grimpuss escapade life had been quite dull. Funny, she usually liked the winter, everything so dingy and deadly, but this winter seemed a bit too miserable and the bats and rats and the rest of the gang were hibernating and waiting for better weather. No entertainment there...

She wrote a brief note of acceptance and posted it

off to Grimolive. *I'll have to give her a wedding present, I suppose,* she grumbled. *And I'm not going to succumb and give her any of that ghastly stuff that she fancies nowadays. No way!*

A few days later she was surprised to hear the phone ringing. She hadn't told anyone about it – except Ev of course. But it was Grimolive!

"I didn't know you'd got the phone in, dear – I was going to write and then, I don't know, something made me ask Directory Enquiries and there you were. I'm so pleased – we'll be able to have nice chats quite often now." Grimolda shuddered. "I do feel you lead an awfully lonely life up there, dear, and a chat sometimes helps." Grimolda squirmed.

"Come to the point, Grimolive," she said.

"Oh yes, dear, well I was just thinking," a momentary silence, "I'm delighted that you're coming, I really am, but you see, you're the only member of the family that I've invited as everyone else is so far away, and they haven't seen me since I moved house and they don't know what I'm doing really – of course I shall write to them all after the wedding and explain. You're the only one who is in on my new life as it were, so I'd love you to be there, but well, I don't know quite how to put it..."

"I know, you're worried I'll give the show away," said Grimolda.

"Well yes, dear. You won't, will you? It would make me so unhappy, and Arthur would never marry me if he knew, and I'd lose all my friends." Olive sounded near to tears.

"Of course I won't, silly," snapped Grimolda, and

thought, *That's a laugh – I'm regretting accepting her invitation and she's regretting inviting me!* That of course made her all the more determined to go. "Don't worry, Grimolive, I'll keep it under my hat," and she cackled at her own joke.

"Oh Mouldy dear, please don't wear your hat! And please could you not wear clothes that make you look like a..."

"A witch," cackled Grimolda. Silly woman can't bring herself to say the word!

"And – and – please don't call me Grimolive either. No-one here knows me by that name. It's really not – not – suitable."

"No, *dear*," said Grimolda sarcastically, and put the phone down, leaving Grimolive in a worse state than ever. She had wanted to have some family at the wedding, but had she done the right thing, or was she heading for total disaster?

Ev drove up to 'The Nettles' at 10 a.m. sharp. His car was sparkling in the sunshine as it had been scrubbed and polished for the occasion, and so had Ev – he looked very smart in his grey suit. For some reason unknown to him he had even put on a grey shirt instead of the pink one he had laid out the night before, and his tie was black and grey with a silver motif.

Grimolda looked at him with approval as she opened the door. Ev, on the other hand, gasped and had to look again. He couldn't believe his eyes. Even in the shadows she looked a different person and when she stepped out into the sunshine he was speechless. She was wearing a trim, slim black suit, black stockings, high-heeled black shoes, and her lanky hair had been tied back and packed under a large-brimmed picture hat, also black. She did look rather as if she was going to a funeral instead of a wedding, but she was so elegant that she could have walked off the cover of *Vogue* magazine.

She even had make-up on! Green eyeshadow and a rather virulent purple lipstick.

"Oh, Miss Grizz," gasped Ev. "You do look terrific!"

And Grimolda actually blushed.

As he opened the car door for her, he came to his senses. There was something he had meant to say.

"Oh by the way – I hope you don't mind. But I've taken the liberty of booking us in at the George and Dragon for the night." Grimolda stopped short. "Really it would be most advisable – one can't drink and drive these days you know, and anyway we would be terribly late home. So you'll need an overnight bag."

"Oh all right," grumbled Grimolda grudgingly, and went back inside.

The drive down the motorway was very pleasant. It was a lovely sunny day, with just a hint of frost, which would no doubt suit Grimolive – Olive – nicely. Grimolda would have preferred a good display of lightning and a massed band of thunder. But she did enjoy the journey and it was fascinating being down on the ground and moving swiftly – quite different from her usual mode of travel and viewpoint. A lot less draughty too! She could get used to this, and was almost tempted to buy a car.

She felt she hadn't a care in the world, and she had left Grimpuss in charge of things back home so didn't need to worry about leaving her home for a couple of days...

They reached Hemingway in plenty of time for lunch, which Ev was quite determined to have, as he didn't want to be drinking on an empty stomach. He had always found that the most enjoyable part of a wedding was the booze and he wasn't intending this to be an exception. He was especially partial to champagne.

"We'll have lunch at the Drunken Duck," said he, pulling up outside the said pub. "I've been here before. Their food's very good."

Grimolda added the name of the pub to her collection of idiotic names that people gave things, that included pigs that flew, and kitties that weren't. Drunken Duck indeed!!

As they came out after a very good lunch of smoked eel, sweetbreads and spinach, sardines on toast, and Gorgonzola cheese, it wasn't only the duck that was drunk. They had each had two martinis before the meal, then ordered a litre of red wine, of which Grimolda had consumed the larger part (Ev was saving up for the champagne) and then they had had a double brandy with their coffee. Ev wasn't too bad but Grimolda was finding that this drink was going straight to her head. Her own brews were far more intoxicating, but she was used to them. She'd never experienced this kind before.

She was having great difficulty forming consonants, and every so often things drifted away in a kind of haze. She had to hang onto Ev's arm as they walked down the street to the registry office, her high heels not doing too well on the cobbles. They reached their destination without incident and in fact rather early as there was no-one else there, and the door was locked. So they stood there, propping each other up and swaying gently, unaware that they were being eyed with curiosity by passers-by, the most imaginative of whom thought they might be the bride and groom!

Chapter Thirteen

After a bit they were joined by one or two well-wishers from Olive and Arthur's council estate, who also eyed the inebriated pair with curiosity. Then Arthur arrived with his best man, a cardboard replica of Arthur, thought Grimolda groggily, and giggled. Arthur smiled at everyone and the two men went inside.

Then the bride's car drew up. The little crowd waved and cheered, and out stepped Olive and her matron of honour, all dressed in bright pink, including the car, which had pink streamers flying from it.

Olive had had her hair freshly permed and it frizzed out under a little pink hat shaped like a rose, with a veil which just covered the tip of her long nose. Her gloves were pink, her shoes were pink, and she carried a posy of pink carnations tied with a pink satin ribbon.

Grimolda, at this sight, was inclined to giggle more than ever, but, pulling herself together, she stepped forward. "Olive, daaahling," she gushed.

Olive backstepped and peered at her, puzzled. She lifted up her veil to see better. Surely, surely this wasn't...

"Yesh, itsh me!" gushed Grimolda, and gave her a big hug.

"Mouldy..." her voice faltered, and no words would come, as she gaped at the vision in front of her.

"Well, whwhatrryouwaitingfor?" grinned Mouldy. "Gwonin an' get hitched," and she gave her a playful push, giggling madly as she thought, *I nearly said 'witched!'*

Olive, who seemed at a loss to know what to do, was then taken in hand by her matron of honour, who led her inside, followed by the little group.

And so Olive and Arthur were married, and lived happily ever after – we hope – but our story doesn't end there. After all there was still the wedding reception to come – and the champagne.

For a small party the George and Dragon was bursting at the seams. The whole neighbourhood must have been there. Of course Arthur had lived there all his life, and Olive, with her sunny disposition, had soon made lots of friends. Champagne flowed and everyone sat down to a generous feast of bland and innocuous food, such as chicken, which Grimolda normally couldn't stand, but she was too far gone to notice what she was eating. After the meal a group appeared, to provide music for dancing. They looked vaguely familiar, but Grimolda couldn't think where she might have seen them before, and she forgot to think about it as she listened to the toe-tapping music. Soon she was gyrating on the dance floor as enthusiastically as everyone else.

At a lull in the proceedings Olive came over to their table with Arthur. "We haven't had the pleasure of being introduced to your friend," she smiled at Ev.

"Ev... Ev Peabody," said Ev quickly, shaking hands with both of them and getting in before Miss Grizz could say 'Evelyn'. "So pleased to meet you, and I hope you'll both be very happy."

"Thank you," beamed Olive, "and I hope you're enjoying yourselves."

"Shwonderful occashun," gushed Grimolda.

"I didn't realise that was your cousin," said Arthur as they walked away. "I hardly recognised her. Doesn't she look smart! Everyone is asking if she comes from London. I didn't notice her lisp before."

Olive couldn't get over how charming Mouldy was today, as well as how smart she looked. Perhaps this Ev person had helped her turn over a new leaf. She seemed to have lost her absent-mindedness and she didn't seem in the least senile. *I've been misjudging her,* she thought. *And she looks years younger than her old self. A nice young man,* Olive thought, *a bit young for her, but does that matter nowadays? Now I wonder...* And little plans and ideas began to form in her head, to be rudely interrupted by Mouldy's voice shouting her name. She turned and went back.

"I nearly forgot, dear," said Mouldy, "I've got your wedding preshent, and I'd better give it to you before you go off on your," she nudged Olive and winked, "honeymoon. Itsh in my bedroom. Come up and get it now, dear," and she grabbed Olive by the arm and bustled her over to the stairs.

"How kind of you, Mouldy," said Olive, quite nonplussed by this new image of her cousin.

"There wash no point in shending it, when we were coming. It would have cosht an arm and a leg to post," and she giggled again as she turned the key in the door. There on the bed stood a huge brown paper parcel. Olive hugged her cousin and eagerly untied the string and the paper fell apart to reveal – a large pink pig!

"Shtuffed it myshelf," said Grimolda proudly. "And itsh your favourite colour."

"Er thank you dear... it's er... lovely," gasped Olive, when she could get the words together, as she tried to cover her horror with a smile. "I'll just wrap it up again, shall I, and go and put it in the boot of the car."

Where and how am I going to hide it from Arthur? she thought with a shudder. *It's hideous!*

When they came back downstairs, Ev was waiting for Grimolda at their table. "I've ordered a bottle of champagne for us," he beamed, indicating the bottle in its bucket of ice. "Mustn't mix our drinks, eh, what? Nothing quite like it," and he proceeded to pour out a large glass for each of them.

It was this champagne that did the final damage. Ev got more and more intoxicated but Mouldy was – to put it politely – paralytic. Luckily for a while it stopped her talking altogether as there's no saying what might otherwise have happened to her vocabulary, and she danced about with a silly grin on her face. At one point Ev had to restrain her forcibly from dancing on the table.

It was getting late, the happy couple were long gone, and most of the guests had departed; Mouldy and Ev were the only wedding guests who were staying overnight and he was getting worried. How was he going to get her sobered up enough to be able to undress herself and go to bed? He certainly wasn't going to oblige!

"How about a bit of fresh air, Miss Grizz?" he said. "A walk before we turn in?"

"Shure, Ev, shuper," and she staggered out hanging onto him.

Once out in the cool night air, she seemed to find her voice again, and now he couldn't stop her talking.

"Shluvly party, Ev," she kept saying as they staggered along. They stopped at the bridge and leaned on the parapet. Looking up, there was the moon and, looking down, there was the moon, staring back at them from the inky black mirror of water beneath.

"I should be there," said Mouldy, pointing down. "No there," and she pointed up. "I should be flying about up there, inshtead of walking about down here. I don't like walking. Will you come wish me?"

Ev laughed and hiccupped. That didn't seem quite right somehow.

"We can't get up there – I don't think," he said vaguely.

"Oh yesh we can," said Grimolda.

"Oh no we can't," chanted Ev.

"Oh yesh we can," sang Grimolda.

This little game went on for a bit until Grimolda suddenly exclaimed, "Oh no we can't." Ev looked at her. She wasn't playing fair. "I'she not got my shtick," said Grimolda in explanation.

"You need the plane as well," said Ev, thinking of course of joysticks rather than broomsticks.

"No, no, no, NO," said Grimolda, shaking her head. "Don't need a plane. Wishes don't need planesh."

"No, thas true," said Ev, "I often wish I could float about in the air. It would save an awful lot of shoe leather!"

"No not you. You're not a wish," said Grimolda, emphasising what she was saying by tapping him on the chest. "It'sh me. *I'm* the wish," and she redirected the tapping at herself.

"You can't be a wish. People can *have* wishes, they can't *be* wishes." Ev, in his fuddled state, couldn't think how to explain it to her in her fuddled state.

"No, no, not a wish – a *wish*," said Mouldy emphatically. You know, *wish*. Big black hat and cloak with a broomshtick, flying about cashting shpellls kind of wish."

Ev laughed heartily. "I like it," he said. "Thas very funny, that is. If you were a witch I'd be a wizard! Wouldn't tha' be great. I wouldn't need to go to work any more. Jus' sit aroun' all day casting spells," and he started dancing round Mouldy, waving his hands and chanting "Abracadabra, abracadabra, abracadabradoo, bubble bubble toil and trouble, whee whee whoo!"

Grimolda felt quite insulted. He wasn't taking her seriously. She was just going to do something to prove her point when something seemed to float in the air across her line of vision. It was a ghostly shadow of Grimolive, wailing, "Please don't give the show away!" Mouldy sighed. Was Olive always going to turn up to spoil her fun?

Anyway she didn't have any spell-making equipment with her, so she contented herself with wishing herself a few inches off the ground as her feet were hurting something awful; besides she was finding it very difficult to keep herself upright.

"I thing we've had enough fresh air," she said and as Ev agreed and turned and wobbled back, she floated along beside him, quite pleased that she hadn't entirely forgotten who she was.

The next day, Arthur caught Olive trying to smuggle the brown paper parcel from the car boot to the shed, in the hope that she could hide it there. Their cases sat waiting in the hall – they were all packed and ready to leave for their honeymoon in Marbella.

"What's this?" he asked.

Caught in the act, Olive could only tell the truth. "It's a wedding present, Arthur. But it's not really very suitable. I wasn't going to show it to you."

"Well then you'll have to now, my girl," said Arthur. "Bring it into the living room and let's have a dekko."

He carried it in for her and stood back as she unwrapped it in trepidation.

"Why that's marvellous!" he exclaimed. "What a lovely bit of work!"

Olive looked at him in amazement.

"Didn't you know, dear? The pig's my family emblem. My family have always been proud of having a family crest. 'Strong roots', our motto is. What a clever idea for a present. Who's it from?"

"My cousin Mouldy," stuttered Olive, not quite believing her ears.

"Well, she must be psychic," said Arthur.

At that moment Mouldy and Ev were returning home rather more sedately than they had come. Both of them were feeling extremely fragile and Ev was saying, "Gosh we did go our dinger last night, didn't we, Mouldy?" He hadn't even known her first name before last night – probably a pet name for Mildred, he thought – but now he felt quite justified in using it. "I was completely blotto, I was. All I can remember is that we seemed to be either wanting to fly about in the sky or float about with our feet off the ground – I even thought we were! And you were going on about being a..." As he looked sideways at Grimolda he thought, *No, I can't tell her, the old soul – she looks too like one as it is. I must have imagined it all anyway*, and he said instead, "You were going on about wishes being able to come true."

"I'm afraid I don't really remember anything about last night," lied Mouldy, having the grace to blush as she stared straight ahead.

She had no intention now of making him any the wiser about something that had been just a laughing matter to him.

And there and then she made a firm resolution never again to drink any unfamiliar alcohol, especially champagne. Apart from anything else, what horrified her most about the effect it had had on her, was that it had totally changed her personality. It had almost turned her into another Olive!

And she shivered at the thought of a fate worse than death.

"Don't you ever again give me champagne, Ev Peabody," she said severely.

"No ma'am," said Ev, not entirely sure that he meant it. In his opinion it had been the making of the old dear!

Chapter Fourteen

Meanwhile, back at the ranch Grimpuss was feeling very disgruntled and left out. He was furious with Grimolda for going off with Ev and leaving him behind, even though she had left him in charge, and asked him to make sure to look after everything in her absence. He should have felt important, but he just felt depressed.

In a huff, he didn't even wave them off but sat in the kitchen, staring at the black charred embers in the fireplace. They reflected his mood to a Tee.

After a while he stomped out of the house and aimlessly drifted along, bumping into trees until he found himself at the edge of the wood at The Nettles' boundary wall. He leapt up and sat looking around him. Immediately below him was the garden and house which had provided him with such good entertainment the last time he had felt ignored by his mistress.

Mr Smith, the owner, just happened to be sitting at a table in the garden, very busily tapping away on a small object on the table in front of him. At that moment a phone rang inside the house, and as it kept ringing and no-one seemed to be thinking of answering it, he heaved a sigh and went inside, leaving the little box on the table.

Grimpuss perked up. The man seemed to be in the middle of a long conversation – he could hear his voice droning on. Galvanised into action, he leapt off the wall and grabbed Mr Smith's plaything between his front paws and flew back to the wall.

Over the years he had worked on his art of leaping from tree to tree to such an extent that he could actually fly for short distances. Being a witch's cat probably helped!

This was a perfect opportunity for him to apply this skill and off he went. From the wall he leapt/flew to the top of the nearest tree, from where he had a perfect view into his neighbour's garden.

Mr Smith came back into the garden and stood for a minute, staring at the bare table. He turned and shouted to his wife, who came out of the house looking bemused as he accused her of removing his iPad. A heated argument ensued and the couple went back indoors, getting very worked up, while Grimpuss smirked up on his lofty perch.

Now he was presented with a problem. With the couple inside the house he could no longer entertain himself. What to do now? Best to take his prize back to his house and find out more about it. Since Grimolda's purchase of the television he had developed an interest in technology, so he was keen to learn what magic this little item held.

The screen was set at an Amazon website, it said. Mr Smith had been in the middle of buying something. All the details were there including his Visa number and personal details – he had been about to complete the deal when Grimpuss commandeered it. It said he had ordered two garden cushions. Another box said 'continue shopping', and 'add to your basket'. As a whole lot of other garden furniture items now appeared listed below, Grimpuss thought, *Great, I can play around,* and he proceeded to tap on everything he saw, which then seemed to register as another item to buy. 'Continue shopping' kept appearing on the screen, and then 'proceed to check out' and 'confirm order'.

He had now also ordered a swing hammock seat, two recliner chairs, all with matching pattern covers, a garden parasol, a picnic hamper, as well as the original order, which had been for the cushions for his existing garden chairs. *This is going to be fun*, thought Grimpuss, as he added them to the basket and booked for next day delivery.

Of course, he would have to be there to watch the Smiths' reaction when this all arrived!

Next day he was up early, all bright-eyed and bushy-tailed, and set off for his vantage point on the wall. His ears pricked up when a delivery van appeared in front of the house, but the house was blocking his view, so he boldly jumped down into the garden (luckily there was no sign of the Smiths' cat) and hid behind a bush at the side of the house. He still couldn't see much, but he could hear quite clearly the raised voice of Mrs Smith protesting that there was some mistake. The delivery man ignored her protests and just kept dumping all these packages in front of her. "Maybe your husband ordered them as a surprise. Just sign here, please," and he jumped into his van and drove off.

Into the house she went and Grimpuss heard Mrs Smith shouting as she accused her husband of "ordering a lot of junk!" which of course he denied.

"You must have had a 'senior moment'," she said. "Probably why you also mislaid your iPad,"

"Well," he said, "at least it will cheer up the garden! Give me a hand and help me carry it all through to the back."

Grimpuss scampered back to his wall, feeling rather deflated. The outcome wasn't quite what he had expected. It had all backfired.

He decided to go back to the house and see what else he could do with this clever iPad, only to discover there was a problem. The only reason he'd achieved what he had was because it was already primed to send an order. When he opened it up he discovered that he couldn't do anything without a password, which of course he didn't know. He was pretty cheesed off. It was useless without Mr Smith's input!

He might as well just return it, so he nipped back to the Smiths' garden while it was empty of owners and cat, and replaced it where he had found it, on the table. So much for that bright idea!

The next day of course he was expecting the return of his mistress. While he was waiting he thought he would pop down to see how his neighbours were getting on, hoping that he would at least find them still rowing. To his chagrin there they were, reclining on their new loungers with glasses of wine and nibbles from the picnic hamper, and listening to soft music playing from their iPad, the cat curled up on a cosy cushion. All blissfully happy.

Grimpuss was not amused! He was even more disgruntled than before!

Chapter Fifteen

As they trundled along her drive in Ev's car, Grimolda decided she was actually happy to see her old home again and was looking forward to settling down to her old life. Things had really been getting a bit too exciting and out of hand. She just wasn't used to all the excitement, and she had mixed feelings about Ev. He had been really good company, but was she becoming too accustomed to being with him?

She thanked him for taking her to her cousin's wedding and waved him off with vague murmurs of keeping in touch. Off he went. He'd been hoping he'd be invited in for a cuppa and chat about their adventures. It was a bit of an anti-climax just sent off like this. He realised he was going to miss Mouldy, and was quite surprised!

Grimpuss welcomed her with effusive purrs – you would think she had been away for weeks! And everything seemed to be just the way she had left it, she was relieved to find.

In no time her trip seemed quite dreamlike as she settled into her old ways. Well, not quite. No matter how hard she tried, her memory of drinking champagne and actually enjoying it stayed with her. Her taste buds seemed to have been attacked and nothing she drank now could replace the bubbly taste of the champagne!

So much so that she came to the conclusion that 'if you can't beat them, join them'. She would just have to start making her own! She had heard somewhere that gooseberries produced the nearest thing to champagne, home wine makers said. Having made a decision, she felt a lot better, and having a plan made her a bit happier. So she set to, getting together all the apparatus she required, including a book on homemade wine. If humans could do it, so could she!

Some time later she tasted the results of her work. Yuck! Nothing like the flavour she remembered. Maybe she should rely on her own powers. Off she went round her garden looking for other ingredients to add. Eventually she was happier with the fruits of her labours.

She sat back, exhausted but pleased with her work. It wasn't quite the same as the taste of champagne that she remembered, but she reckoned it was pretty close. She was so pleased with her efforts that she thought she should get someone else's opinion.

Of course! The obvious person to taste her wine was Ev! She immediately went off to get her phone. Ev was in, and really interested in her exploits and keen to taste her wine. "I could pop along now if you like."

"That would be brilliant, Ev." He was so pleased to hear from her and he was beginning to miss her company – there had never been a dull moment in their trip.

When he arrived, Grimolda took him into her front room – the occasion seemed to merit special treatment. She handed him a glass of her 'champagne'. Ev took a tentative sip. "Mmmm," he murmured, and took another, and another. "This is really good," he said. "It doesn't actually taste like champagne to me, but it is delicious! And it's very bubbly! How did you manage to get it tasting so mature when it's so new?"

Grimolda couldn't possibly say that she had used a spell or two to speed up the process. "It's just the ingredients I used, and that's my secret!"

"I have an idea," said Ev, "I should really take a bottle along to my local pub, and see what the landlord thinks. Would you mind? "

Grimolda agreed. She was chuffed that Ev thought it tasted so good. "But just say that it's a secret recipe, passed down through generations?"

For the next day or two Grimolda was on tenterhooks and kept eyeing the phone, willing it to ring. Instead of its usual place in the cellar, it now sat on her kitchen table.

At last it did ring. She grabbed it – it had to be Ev. No-one else ever phoned. "Well?" she almost shrieked down the phone.

"Great news!" he exclaimed. "George loves it! And he'd like to sell it for you – sale or return. Is that possible? Do you have enough to supply him with, if he wants to add it to his regular stock?"

"Oh yes, I've got gallons of the stuff already. It's no problem. What about a label?"

"I could run them off on my computer. What are you going to call it?"

"How about 'SHAMPAGNE'?!" This appealed to her sense of humour! Ev wasn't so sure.

"What about 'THE NETTLES SPECIAL' or 'SPOOKEY HEATH PRIME TIME'? I'll see what George says."

Grimolda felt energised and immediately set about bottling what she had already made, and making some more. She was glad she had made a note of the ingredients and amounts. It wouldn't do if they all tasted differently. Although that did appeal to her sense of humour too. She could have called it 'POT LUCK'?! No, better not!

Amazingly George's reply was that he liked 'SHAMPAGNE'! So Ev started on the labels right away.

After a session spent sticking on some labels, they were ready. "We should just start with a dozen, to see what other people think, and I think you should come with me to meet George." Grimolda agreed grudgingly. She would have preferred to remain incognito.

They arrived at the Bear and Ball. Grimolda was relieved to see that it was quite quiet, not yet time for the pre-lunch crowd. Ev introduced her. George was a bit taken aback. This lady was not at all like what he expected, although he wasn't quite sure what he had expected. Dressed all in black, and with her sharp features she was a forbidding presence. But he was the one selling the wine, she didn't have to be there. He just hoped she wouldn't become a regular customer! Anyway they agreed a deal and had a glass of Grimolda's 'shampagne' to celebrate.

Their journey home was a very cheerful one. Ev was pleased with their success so far, and Mouldy was pleased at her success. All that remained was the effect it was going to have on the public.

Two days later Ev phoned to say that George had phoned him to say that the wine was a great success – he had sold all twelve bottles they had left with him, and could he have some more please!

"No problem," said Grimolda, "I've plenty more bottled up and ready."

"Shall I come and fetch you later today? And maybe take twenty this time?"

And so another trip to the Bear and Ball was made. This time they left with a cash payment for the wine sold. Grimolda wanted to give Ev a share, but he said she should have it all. "After all, it's your creation, your baby!"

All the way home in his car, Grimolda was scheming, and once he dropped her off, allowing him a few minutes to get on his way, she tripped gaily down the drive and walked to the nearest little shopping arcade and bought herself a bottle of real champagne – the same she had enjoyed at

Grimolive's wedding, and carried it home carefully.

She couldn't admit to Ev that she had been trying to make champagne as good as the real champagne, and although the invented wine was nice it wasn't a patch on the 'Real McCoy'! Settled back in her rocking chair, she poured herself a glass, then another, then another. "Yummy scrumptious," she muttered. "This will have to be my secret!"

As she rocked contentedly she thought back to the time not so long ago when she was bored out of her mind, grumbling about her life in this modern world. And look at what had happened since. Her life had changed so much, so much had happened, and here she was, she couldn't remember ever being so happy, and it wasn't just the drink talking. She grinned at Grimpuss in his corner, and he grinned back, not quite knowing why, but he might as well humour the old dear. He was surprised to find that he was really happy too!

Printed in Great Britain
by Amazon.co.uk, Ltd.,
Marston Gate.